THE CHAMBER OF THE ANCIENTS

WRAK-WAVARA: THE AGE OF DARKNESS
BOOK TWO

LEIGH ROBERTS

DRAGON WINGS PRESS

CONTENTS

Editing by Joy Sephton http://www.justemagine.biz
Cover design by Cherie Fox http://www.cheriefox.com

Sexual activities or events in this book are intended for adults.

ISBN: 978-1-951528-23-2 (ebook)
ISBN: 978-1-951528-25-6 (paperback)

Dedication

*To hearts, though weary, who still find the courage
to ask—*

What If?

CHAPTER 1

Pan bolted upright. *Where am I? What just happened?*

As she threw back her sleeping hide, she froze. Her father's heavy Leader's Staff was propped up in one of the corners. *Oh no.*

She hurried directly to her parents' quarters, rushing down the tunnel as quietly as she could because it was so early. The door was open as if inviting anyone in. She called out, and when there was no answer, entered the room and quickly scanned the interior.

Her parents were gone.

The sleeping mat was arranged tidily with nothing awry except that the red jasper her mother always kept by her bedside was missing. Moc'Tor had given the stone to E'ranale as a reminder not only of the divine love of the Great Spirit but also of his love for her.

And of course, the corner where the 'Tor Leader's Staff always leaned was empty.

Pan dashed from the room and down the corridors of Kthama to find her brother, Dak'Tor. She called out his name as she snatched up and slammed the announcement stone on his door. The rock shattered, and pieces flew everywhere. "Dak'Tor! Wake up, wake up. Something terrible has happened!"

It took a moment before Dak'Tor pulled the door open and peered at her. "What is wrong? What are you shouting about?"

"Mother and Father are gone. Their room is empty, and I had such a strange dream—" Her voice trailed off, and she did not mention the Leader's Staff. Dak'Tor was supposed to be the next Leader of the High Rocks, not her.

"We must find our sisters, come on," she said.

Shortly, all four were assembled. Pan took her siblings to their parents' quarters so they could see for themselves. She waited, biting her tongue while the others took in the scene.

"Where is the Leader's Staff?" asked Dak'Tor.

Pan hesitated. Oh no. How could she tell him their father had chosen her to lead? But she must. She hoped he would not be crushed.

"It was in my room when I woke up," she said quietly.

"Mother and Father are gone, and the Leader's Staff is in your quarters." Dak'Tor repeated her words as if he was still not fully awake.

"I know, but I do not want to lead, Dak'Tor. If Father is truly gone, then you are heir to the leadership of the High Rocks, not me," Pan said.

"But if Father left the staff in your quarters, then you have been chosen to be Adik-Tar," pointed out her sister, Inrion.

"I *do not* wish to lead. Father and I talked about it, and I was under the impression it would fall to our brother."

Dak'Tor finally spoke. "I have no hard feelings. I admit that you are more qualified than I. You are a Guardian, like Father."

Pan shook her head. It was enough responsibility that she was Guardian.

"Why are we talking about this? Enough! We can come back to it later," Pan said. "Did any of you also experience anything peculiar last night while you were sleeping?"

All three nodded.

"Tell me what happened," Pan said.

"It was dark, and then a ring of faces appeared," Vel answered. "And it was more real than anything I have ever dreamed about. I do not even know where I was, only that I was watching something unfold. They did not really speak, but there clearly was a message that seemed to be for the Akassa. For some reason, I can remember it clearly.

"*We are Mothoc. We are keepers of the Others. What had to be done was done. But no more. Never again, the Wrak-Wavara. The Others who are our wards are now your Brothers. Learn their language. Make amends. Regain their trust. Leader to next Leader. Kthama Healer to next Kthama Healer. Only these may speak of this past. This is Rah-hora. We leave you to the future of your own making. When the Wrak-Ayya falls, the Age of Shadows, the true test will begin. We will be watching.'"*

"I had exactly the same dream," said Inrion wonderingly as Dak'Tor nodded his agreement. "It was so powerful. And there was another message for the Sassen, similar but not quite. Both ended the same. *We will be watching.* That sounds as if they are still here. But where?"

"Kthama Minor?" exclaimed Vel.

The 'Tor siblings quickly made their way down the winding overgrown path to Kthama Minor. But as they came around the corner to where the entrance should have been, there was no opening. Instead, a massive rock of unimaginable size was firmly lodged in the entrance. It was pressed against the towering cliff and embedded partially into the wall itself.

Kthama Minor had somehow been sealed.

Higher up than anyone could reach, a symbol had been carved into the front of the stone. Seeing the mark, they turned questioningly to Pan.

"Wrak-Wavara. It is the symbol for Wrak-Wavara, the Age of Darkness," she said.

Faint shimmering energy bathed the entire area.

Kthama Minor had not only been sealed, but its essence had been cloaked.

Finally, Pan spoke again. "Kthama Minor is no longer ours. She and her secrets now belong to the past. The message is clear. So be it."

Then Pan grew silent and stilled. She reached her mind down into the vortex and harnessed the power of the Aezaitera. Deeply connected to the creative life force, she coaxed a profusion of thick woody vines to grow over the face of the huge rock, completely hiding the mark of Wrak-Wavara. The others, who had not seen her publicly demonstrate her Guardian abilities, stood in awe.

Taking one last look at where the entrance had been, Pan said, "Come. Kthama Minor and the Age of Darkness must disappear from our history so that we are never tempted to repeat these crimes again. In our sleep, we all witnessed the Rah-hora."

The siblings silently turned their backs on Kthama Minor, and walked away, each lost in their own thoughts and feelings.

It did not take long for the Akassa Leader, Takthan, to seek out Pan. He brought with him an Akassa female named Tensil, who had been studying under Tyria to become a Healer. Tyria had suggested that the Akassa would benefit from an additional Healer, one of their own size.

Takthan'Tor was of direct 'Tor descent from Ny'on's bloodline. Many years before, Ny'on had been Moc'Tor's Second Choice, and in support of Moc'Tor's direction, her daughters and subsequent family females had been seeded by the Others. That line had bred true for many generations, but somehow, despite the heavy influence of the Others' blood, the males of Ny'on's line were the largest and most robust of the Akassa males.

"Guardian, last night I had a strange experience. So did Tensil and many others. We need to talk to you about it."

Pan silently listened while Takthan told her what she already knew. When he was done speaking, they agreed to call the Akassa together. They could not pretend such a mystical event had not happened.

Takthan understood the power of the Rah-hora, a sacred vow of honor that once formed could not be broken without severe consequences. He would faithfully carry out what had been asked of him.

That done, Pan called a meeting of the Mothoc of Kthama. They stood crowded together around what, only the day before, had been the opening to Kthama Minor.

All could tell that Kthama Minor had been cloaked, could feel the faintly shimmering field that would be below the Akassa's threshold of perception.

"It is true then," said Nisere, looking up at the giant stone sealing the entrance. "Is this why you have called us here, Pan?"

"Yes. Please, speak freely. Tell me what you have each experienced since yesterday."

The others talked openly about the dream.

After much discussion, Pan spoke once more. "We all had the same dream. It appears that the Akassa are now charged with making peace with the Others, which leads me to believe that the Akassa are meant at some point to step into leadership. As for the past, Takthan and Tensil may speak of it rarely and only between themselves and the Akassa Leaders to come. And from now on, we, the Mothoc, must do the same, to let the past die."

Then Pan could no longer avoid saying the words she did not want to say, "You should know that my parents are both missing. Their quarters are empty, and we do not know where they went. Our mother was deathly ill, and whatever has happened, I believe she no longer walks Etera. As for my father, I do not know. Whatever has happened to him seems to be beyond my perception, even as a Guardian."

There was much murmuring before anyone spoke again. Dochrohan turned to Dak'Tor. "So you now lead Kthama."

Dak'Tor said nothing, but looked at Pan.

"That is not clear at the moment," she said firmly.

Dochrohan stared at them but said no more about it. "So the past needs to slip from the memory of the Akassa. But that will take generations, and how do we even enforce it? Does forbidding them to speak of it not simply create more interest? We cannot stop whisperings in private."

"Our culture is their culture. They will not violate the Rah-hora." Pan noticed Tyria shifting back and forth. "Do you wish to add anything?"

"No, but I would like to speak with you alone," she answered.

"Very well. If there are no more questions, let us dismiss. Tonight I will address all of the High Rocks. And I must also let everyone else know that my parents are gone. Then I will reach out to the High Council to see how pervasive this experience was."

After everyone had left, Pan turned expectantly to Tyria.

"I have said I had the same dream, Guardian, though we know that is not what it really was—but there is more. I was given information to be handed down only from Healer to Healer—and only by those at Kthama. I do not believe I am allowed to share it with anyone, even you, for which I apologize. The knowledge of the content could affect the future path of the Akassa." she said. "And there is more; it seems that information was also given to Tensil."

"I understand, and I respect your discretion. It seems to affirm that at some point, Tensil will become a Healer in her own right."

Together, Pan and Tyria strolled back to Kthama.

"How everything can change so quickly, I do not

know," Pan said as they parted company. "Get some rest; the days ahead will no doubt be trying."

After nightfall, all those living at the High Rocks stood assembled in the Great Chamber. Pan stood at the front with her siblings. Tyria was standing in the front row, as Pan had asked her to. It was the first time the young Guardian had spoken from her father's place of leadership. She first scanned the sea of faces looking back at her, now clearly either Akassa or Mothoc.

All eyes were on her as she began. "People of the High Rocks, I have asked you to come together because we have all experienced an event of mystical proportions. You understand the Rah-hora that has been put in place. You know what is required of you. I remind you of your duty to play your part. I will not speak of it again; after tonight, let no one speak of the past. What is done is done. Let us move together into the future of our making."

She stopped to look at the faces in the crowd.

"There is more I must tell you. A great loss has befallen Kthama. My parents, Moc'Tor and E'ranale, are no longer with us. We awoke this morning to find their quarters empty. I cannot tell you where they are as we have no idea. You know that my mother was very ill, but whatever has happened to them may forever be a mystery. I know this is difficult, as it also is for my siblings and me. If I had answers, I would give them to you."

Pan watched the sea of faces ripple as everyone glanced around. "What do you mean? Where are they?" a voice called out from the crowd.

"I do not know where they are," Pan replied. "All I can truly tell you is that they are no longer here with us at Kthama."

"Why would they leave us? What does it all mean?"

"How can they just be gone? If they are dead, where are their bodies?"

"Is Dak'Tor Leader of Kthama now?"

Pan looked over at her brother, who stepped forward to speak. "Pan woke up to find our parents gone and the Leader's Staff in her quarters. She will lead Kthama."

"The staff is passed only to the next Leader, so that is right. It must have been Moc'Tor's choice that Pan lead," said another voice.

Dak'Tor stood stoically, unmoving.

Pan frowned at him before raising her hand to quiet them. "Takthan will lead with me. Together, we will face the future with you.

"I realize that the loss of my parents will affect each of us differently. I will not tell you how to grieve; you must each find a way to accept what has happened and move forward. If I learn more, I will share it. Believe me on that."

Abuzz, the crowd took a while to disperse.

The mystery of where Moc'Tor and E'ranale's bodies were would lead to great speculation. Eventually, a rumor would survive that the Great Spirit had somehow, supernaturally, taken them from Etera. The same end as had come to the Guardian who served before Moc'Tor, Wrollonan'Tor.

Once the Great Chamber was emptied, Pan approached Dak'Tor.

"I cannot believe you said that about the Leader's Staff," she scowled. "We had not yet discussed it."

"I do not understand," he replied. "Kthama needs a clear Leader, some stability. Whatever is meant to happen, Takthan is not ready to lead the High Rocks. The people are used to having a Guardian as Leader, so it creates continuity, and, regardless, Father decided to make you the Leader. But if you wish to take it to the High Council and have it overturned—"

Pan rubbed her face with both hands. Their parents were probably dead, and they were arguing over who would lead the High Rocks. She turned and left abruptly; she must send word to the Mothoc Leaders and Healers of the other communities asking for them to come to High Rocks immediately. Not a High Council meeting, Pan needed to speak privately with only her fellow Mothoc.

That night, Pan lay in her quarters on her sleeping mat, replaying the events of the last few years that had led up to this moment. *Where are you, Father?*

She did not understand why she could not sense him. Was Moc'Tor still there somewhere, having cloaked himself even from her ability to discern? But if so, why? And what other powers did a Guardian then have of which she was not aware? Pan was confident that both her parents had gone, and Etera seemed desperately empty without them. She sighed deeply and rolled over. Overcome with grief that her parents were no more and that her father had left her to figure it all out on her own, Pan wrapped herself into a tight ball and prayed for the forgetfulness of sleep.

Days passed before Pan received word back from the other Mothoc Leaders and the Healers. They agreed to her proposed meeting date, and eventually, she stood before them in a clearing not far from Kthama.

The summer heat was in full force, making it uncomfortable for them with their heavy coats. Only the slight breeze gave them any relief, so they stood in the shade of a stand of towering oaks, trying to ignore the insects and the bees buzzing around. Bright red, orange, and white flowers rimmed the clearing, swaying daintily in the light wind. For the first time ever, Pan thought that immersing herself in the cool waters of the Great River might be refreshing.

Looking back at the circle around her, she began. "I asked you to meet here because I did not wish to risk the Akassa overhearing our discussion. As an added precaution, I have also cloaked the area from them, so you may speak freely now.

"There is no doubt we have all witnessed a super-natural intervention, and I have called you together to discuss our plans for moving forward *to the future of our making.*" She used the exact words from the vision, and members of the crowd nodded their affir-mation and understanding.

As she spoke, her eyes roamed the crowd, and standing next to his father, Hatos'Mok, Leader of the Deep Valley, she found her beloved, Rohm'Mok. She denied her desire to look over every inch of him and run into his arms. Instead, she stood in her place as Guardian.

Hatos'Mok was first to speak. "We are aware of what has taken place, Guardian. Some of us here were involved in the Ror'Eckrah, which brought this to pass. It was your father's plan to protect the future of Etera."

The Ror'Eckrah; the sacred joining into the One Mind. "I see. And so you and *who else* were aware of this plan?" Despite her attempts to stifle her reaction, there was a distinct edge to her voice.

Hatos'Mok replied, "The oldest of us here. Those

of the communities' Leaders who led with your father."

"Then you know where my father and mother are?"

"Your father and mother walk Etera no longer, Guardian. Their bodies are sealed inside a small chamber within Kthama Minor."

Pan squeezed her eyes shut. *Robbed even of the chance to say goodbye.*

"If I may explain," Hatos'Mok took a step forward and regarded all four siblings. "Your father knew this would be hard on all of you.

"Above everything else, Moc'Tor felt his responsibility to Etera. He worked hard not to let his personal feelings interfere with what he saw as his duty. He knew you were struggling in particular with the difficulties of your—your mother's situation. Your father asked me, before the Ror'Eckrah fell into place, to give you an explanation. To spare you from feelings of guilt for taking part in their passing, he intentionally did not involve any of you. He was also concerned that, in addition to the guilt, your emotional involvement might unwittingly create interference with the process. Or that you might have tried to stop him enacting the plans for himself and your mother, plans that E'ranale also agreed to."

Pan looked at Dak'Tor, Vel, and Inrion, who all wore the same pained expression she imagined was on her own face. She clasped her hands behind her back and dug her nails into her palms.

The group fell quiet, giving Pan and her siblings a moment to work through the new information. Only the rustling of the breeze through the treetops broke the silence.

"Is this your assumption," she challenged Hatos'Mok, "of what my father and mother were thinking?"

"No assumption at all, Guardian. Moc'Tor told me this directly before the final steps were put in motion."

Pan remained silent. She could feel small drops of blood from where her nails had pierced her own flesh.

Finally, Tres'Sar of the Far High Hills spoke up. "Guardian, we feel for the pain this has caused you, but it seems you are now Leader of the High Rocks —" He glanced over at Dak'Tor, who was standing in front with Pan.

She pulled herself together. "I am temporarily acting as Leader."

"*Temporarily?*" asked Tres'Sar. He looked at Dak'Tor as if expecting him to speak. When he did not, Tres'Sar addressed him directly, "Do you challenge your sister for the leadership of the High Rocks?"

Dak'Tor spoke up, "No, I do not. I believe that as she is the Guardian, her leadership will provide continuity for Kthama. But, anyway, the question of what I want or do not want is moot. As we know, the Leader's Staff was left in her quarters. Father must have believed she was the best choice to serve along with the Akassa Leader. However, until an Akassa Leader is ready to take over, it will be necessary to keep a Mothoc Leader in place."

"We do not doubt the Guardian's abilities," said Tarris'Kahn, Leader of the small now-nameless community just up the Mother Stream from the High Rocks, the son of their Leader who had recently returned to the Great Spirit. "But—at least toward the end—it seemed a great strain on Moc'Tor to be both Guardian and Leader. However, the Leader's choice of successor has never been over-turned. Nor have we ever believed it should be."

"It is not my choice to lead Kthama," Pan said, throwing a glance in the direction of Dak'Tor, who immediately looked away.

Hatos'Mok erupted. "Enough of this! It is sacri-lege. If the Staff was in your quarters when you awoke, Guardian, then Moc'Tor has handed the mantle of leadership to you. That is the end of it. The mantle has been passed to you, so accept your father's decision, work with the Akassa to share lead-ership, and let us move on to the next order of busi-ness. *Immediately.*"

Pan steeled herself from responding in kind. "I have asked you to come together as we must plan how to help the Akassa move forward. Takthan, the Akassa Leader of the House of 'Tor, has come to me and said that all the Akassa received the message. It was clear that they have an obligation to the Others, whom we betrayed during the Wrak-Wavara and whom they must now refer to as the Brothers. They have been charged with finding a way to introduce themselves to the Others, learn their language, gain their trust." She paused as heads nodded.

"Yes, the Akassa Leader of the House of 'Mok, and others, came forward with the same message," Hatos'Mok said.

All through the group, the other Leader's acknowledged the same events in their communities.

"We rarely had any contact with the Others," Tarris'Kahn added. "Any future with them does belong to the Akassa."

Pan nodded. "I propose we schedule regular meetings to agree on the approach we will take as other matters come before us. For one thing, Kthama needs a Healer's Helper. We are fortunate that Tyria has come to us from Kayerm and is taking the place of Oragur, who left for the Deep Valley. And we have Tensil, an Akassa, apprenticing with her. But if I had my way, each community would have more than one Healer in addition to a Healer's Helper."

Oragur spoke up, Krin at his side. "I told your father I would help train a Healer when one was identified, and that offer stands if you so wish. But I do have an announcement. My daughter, Krin'Onida, is now a Healer—and she wishes to be paired."

Pan looked across at Krin. They were friends, and Pan had missed her deeply. She wanted to ask about Liru but could not in such a public forum.

"That is great news," said Hatos'Mok. "Will she stay at the Deep Valley, since you are already Healer there?"

Krin spoke up. "I am open to moving to another community but would prefer not to."

Pan could not stop herself and took advantage of the discussion to look directly at Rohm'Mok, who had been trying to catch her eye since the assembly began. Her knees almost buckled at her longing to be with him, to feel his arms wrapped around her and draw comfort from his strength.

She refocused with difficulty. "The Wall of Records has been sealed along with Kthama Minor, so we must find a new way to record pairings. However, I have to ask, is it even wise that we, the Mothoc, continue to produce offling?"

"Guardian, if we do not continue to produce offling, what will become of Etera?" Pan's heart warmed at hearing Rohm'Mok's voice rise from the crowd.

"You forget the Sassen," she said quietly. "The preservation of Etera is passing into their hands."

Rohm'Mok stared at Pan as if willing her to read his thoughts.

I know, I know, my love. They would soon enough have time alone together.

"Are you proposing we die out altogether, Guardian?" asked one of the other Leaders.

There was so much to discuss, and the rapidly changing topics were making Pan's head spin. She raised her hand to silence them. She wondered if they understood the significance of losing a Guardian, her father, at so young an age. It was a devastating loss to Etera itself, and here they were seeming to not realize the tragedy of it.

"Let us set this aside for another time. I am still dealing with the loss of my parents, and perhaps my mind is not clear enough at the moment. If Krin wishes to be paired, I leave it to you to find her a suitable choice. Without the Wall of Records, we will have to do our best to keep our bloodlines as clear as possible.

"Oragur, do you have the scroll my father spoke of, the one that Lor'Onida made? The one on which she recorded the laws that were agreed upon before the division?" Pan was thinking that any new agreements should also be recorded on the scroll.

"No. I do not know what became of it. My understanding was that the laws were also to be recorded on the Wall of Records, but as you say, we no longer have access to that."

Pan was dismayed at the news. No longer being able to reach the Wall of Records, the scroll would have been a unifying piece of history, for their communities.

"We must mark them down somehow then, or at least commit them to memory," Pan said. "I suggest that be the focus of our next High Council meeting; how we should record our new decisions, so they do not become confused or lost altogether, and how, from now on, to keep track of pairings. And unless anyone else has anything to discuss, I propose the High Council meets at the next moon."

Dak'Tor suddenly spoke up. "Before we dismiss, I would also like to be paired,"

"Are you asking the High Council to pair you with someone?"

"As I am not Leader, yes, I am asking to be paired. I would like to travel to the other communities, as you did when you were searching for a mate."

Pnatl'Rar of the Little River spoke up, "We have many unpaired females if you would like to visit us."

Pan frowned. "Brother, just remember it was agreed that only the Leader has the right to choose their own mate."

Then she closed the meeting, and the other Leaders and the Healers separated into small groups to continue their conversations. Dak'Tor joined one of them. Pan stood a moment watching him. He was built like their father. Only his coloring told them apart, though Dak'Tor did have a large amount of silver in his coat, covering the top of his head and flowing down his shoulders as far as his hips. Depending on how he stood, he might be mistaken for a Guardian from the back. Pan shook her head and walked off to be joined almost immediately by Rohm'Mok.

"Pan, I need to speak with you privately," he said as he caught up to her.

"Not here," she said, walking casually forward

without looking at him. With everyone milling about, there were few places they could meet where they would be undisturbed, "Can you get away and come to my quarters?"

"Yes. I will find an excuse to break away from my father. I will see you as soon as I can," he whispered, and they parted ways.

❀

Before long, Pan and Rohm'Mok were alone in her quarters, tightly wrapped in each other's arms. She let herself melt into the comfort and security of his embrace.

"I have missed you so," he said, looking down at her. "I have also missed you. But I am still reeling from what has happened. And I do not want to lead Kthama; I am trying to make peace with that, but I cannot. How could my father place such a burden on me?"

Pan looked over to the Leader's Staff, still leaning in the corner. She had not touched it, knowing that to do so would officially pass the mantle to her. She was putting off the inevitable, she knew.

"I understand how you feel," Rohm'Mok agreed. "But you are more than able to lead Kthama, and I am ready to stand proudly at your side."

"Tell me; did you know of my father's plan beforehand? Were you among those who, along with your father, knew this was coming?"

"No. I swear I did not. I only witnessed the message in the dream—as you did."

Pan buried her face in the thick hair covering of his chest and breathed deep his male scent, his warmth soothing her.

"Yield to me, Saraste'," he whispered. "Let me comfort you through your struggles."

She did not answer and gently pulled away from him. "If my brother would lead Kthama, perhaps I could go with you, and you would not have to confront your father. Oh, what am I saying? Have I so quickly forgotten my responsibilities as Guardian? My father would be disappointed in me," she said.

"Your father knew the struggles of leadership as much as anyone. And the Guardian bears the greatest burden. He would not be disappointed in you; he would understand the hardship you are under. You are overwrought and not thinking clearly, which is understandable."

"You must go soon. We cannot risk someone looking for you and discovering us here together. It is very improper, but I could not help myself." She traced her fingers along his lips. He captured them gently in his mouth and ran his tongue over them.

Pan sighed as a well of desire overflowed within her. Then she added, "Please, you must go." It took all her strength to say it.

"Only because you have asked me to. And because you are right; it is not proper that I am here. I would never want to do anything to hurt you or tarnish your reputation." Rohm'Mok gave her a soft, gentle kiss.

After he had left, Pan lay on her sleeping mat, enjoying the lingering feel of his lips brushing hers.

She tossed and turned all night.

CHAPTER 2

Deep within the tunnels of Kayerm, the morning after the message delivered by the Ror'Eckrah, Nox'Tor stirred from his deep sleep and blinked his eyes, trying to awake fully. *That was no dream.* He lay there a moment before he eased himself away from his mate, Kyana, and went in search of Wosot and the Healer, Pagara. He found them outside Kayerm's entrance, already engaged in conversation.

"Where is my father?" asked Nox'Tor.

"I am sorry. Your father left with Tyria for Kthama." Wosot broke the news. "He will not be returning."

"No!" Nox'Tor exclaimed. "It is not true. He will be back. He would not just abandon me like this."

"I am sorry." Wosot stepped forward to put a hand on the younger male's shoulder.

Nox'Tor stepped back, avoiding the gesture.

"How can this be true? I am confused—and I had a disturbing dream last night."

"I also had a peculiar dream," said Wosot. "But it was more than a dream."

The three shared their experiences.

"So, this is what my father and his brother, Moc'-Tor, had planned? To threaten the Sassen with annihilation if they approach the Akassa?"

"The message did not threaten them if they contacted the Akassa; it only said that they are not to," said Pagara.

"*Make no contact with the Akassa lest you yourselves be destroyed*?" Nox'Tor quoted. "Sounds like a threat to me. The message is clear enough, and I can only assume it applies to us as well. We are never to contact the Akassa again. I personally have no problem with that; I am fine with letting the past die. My father already ordered us never to speak of Kthama, anyway. We must make our own way into the future now. I wonder if everyone here had the same dream? Though, as you said, Wosot, it was certainly not merely a dream."

He thought a moment. "I hope that, wherever they are, Laborn, Salus, and the rest of their traitorous band also experienced it."

Nox'Tor and the others soon learned that all the Mothoc and Sassen at Kayerm had experienced the vision and that none of the Sassen could remember the location of Kthama or Kthama Minor. The next day, he met again with Wosot and Pagara the Healer, also choosing to include his mate, Kyana.

(来)

The warm, humid air drifted up off the Great River. Nox'Tor had led them to a favorite spot—a secluded alcove in the river's bend, protected by an outcropping of rock and nicely shaded by the huge locust trees that rimmed it. But the rich abundance of the area was lost in the turmoil created by the strange dream they had all experienced.

Nox'Tor pushed down the anxiety rising within him. *I am left alone to lead, without Father's counsel. What if they do not follow me? What then?* He decided he must be strong like his father and give them no choice. So he gritted his teeth and began.

"It is time for change. Our people have been in turmoil since Ushca's death and Ridg'Sor's execution, so I will be calling an assembly. Now that my father is gone, there is even more upheaval. Worse, with the loss of the rebel band members, our numbers are reduced. Looking back will not help us; we must move forward. Therefore, as part of the announcement about my father's departure, I see no other course but to reverse the decree that females can only be mated by one male. For the moment, I will leave it to the females to choose, but no female may remain unmated, and eventually, every female must mate with more than one male if she is not seeded."

"With all due respect," said Wosot, "I served at your father's side for many years, and he accepted my counsel. I hope that you also will. Considering the enormity of what has just taken place, is this the most important thing to focus on? And what about the bloodlines? Our people split over the need to mix our blood with the Others. We are a small community, and indiscriminate pairings will only worsen the problem of a small population, not fix it."

"You can now refer to me properly, Wosot, as Adik'Tar." The new Leader looked Wosot up and down. "Our bloodline will not survive at all if it does not happen. We can make wise choices, but we can no longer afford to mate only one female to one male."

"What are you saying?" asked his mate Kyana, touching his arm. "Are you telling me you are going to find another female with whom to mate?"

"No, I am saying *you* are to find another female for me to mate. I said it would be the female's choice," Nox'Tor replied.

Kyana looked down, obviously fighting tears. "I do not understand. I agree with Wosot; why this drastic change and why so soon? I thought I was enough for you. I thought you loved me."

"I do love you. Your position as my First Choice is secure," he said and put his arm on her shoulder. Kyana shrugged it off and stepped away, turning her back on him. Wosot frowned as she wiped tears from her eyes.

Nox'Tor sighed, "Also, I want all use of the A'Pozz plant eliminated," he added.

Pagara gasped. "I need that in my medicinal stores. I realize you blame Ushca's death on the A'Pozz, but it was the act of Ridg'Sor that took her, not her use of the plant itself."

"I do not care; it is too dangerous. Now that others know of its abilities, I want none of it around. Who knows who might be poisoned next. That is my decision, Healer. I expect it to be followed," he looked at her sternly.

She looked away, refusing to meet his gaze. Then, looking back, she said, "I realize you are Leader now, but this is a mistake. You will cause needless suffering with this decision." She stared fiercely at him now.

"I have made it clear. Take care of it," Nox'Tor barked.

Wosot spoke up again, "Why all these directives so soon? Do you not think you should wait a while before making such drastic changes? And hurtful ones?" he added, glancing at Kyana, who had retreated into silence.

"Our people have been in turmoil since we came to Kayerm. My father only recently forced the Mothoc rebels to leave, and now he is gone, and no one knows what became of him. On the contrary, what is a little more upheaval? We will settle into quieter times, but this is exactly the time for more change. If the females are too short-sighted to recognize it has to be done, well, that is why a male Leader has to make such decisions."

None of them said anything as together they began to walk away from Nox'Tor.

"Wosot, a moment."

The Leader waited until the females were out of sight before drawing back and punching Wosot directly in the face, catching him off guard and causing him to stumble and fall to the ground.

Nox'Tor stood over Wosot and said, "Do not ever again question my decisions in front of anyone. Is that clear?"

Wosot glared up at him, nursing his sore chin with one hand.

"The next correction will not be so gentle," Nox'Tor said and walked off.

⁂

Despite the fact that Wosot could easily have bested Nox'Tor in a fight, he simply stood up and dusted himself off. What had happened? When had Nox'Tor become such a soltark? Straf'Tor had been a strong Leader, but he had also been wise and considered the counsel of others.

At present, Wosot could see very little of the father in the son. Day two in his reign, and he had already resorted to violence? By attacking Wosot,

Nox'Tor had broken one of the Sacred Laws agreed upon before the division. Wosot feared that they were in for hard times under his leadership.

That afternoon, Nox'Tor stood before the assembled people of Kayerm, standing up on the same hillside, just as his father always had. "People of Kayerm. I am not here to try to explain what we all experienced the night before last, only to say that a time of great change has come upon us. Furthermore, as you know, my father's mate, Ushca, was murdered at the hands of the rebel Ridg'Sor, who subsequently paid for the crime with his life. What you may not know is that my father, Straf'Tor, is no longer with us either. He left willingly but not before telling me that I will now lead Kayerm. The time for looking back has passed. A Rah-hora is sacred, and we are honor-bound to abide by it. From this moment forward, contact with the Akassa, as well as with the Others, is forbidden; there is no room for doubt or negotiation. I will do my best to lead you as my father would have done. In return, I expect the same allegiance from you that you gave him."

Nox'Tor stood for a moment and looked out at the sea of hair-covered bodies and the dark eyes staring back at him, the larger Mothoc and the smaller Sassen. At a loss for anything else to say, Nox'Tor ended the assembly awkwardly by walking off. Many stayed, shocked at both the announcement and that Straf'Tor had abandoned them with no explanation.

※

Almost overnight, the lives of the Akassa and the Sassen had permanently been altered. The Akassa were bound by the Rah-hora to let the past go and to look after the Others, now to be called the Brothers. The Sassen had been forbidden to contact the Akassa and now had no memory of the locations of either Kthama or Kthama Minor. Sassen and Akassa each held part of the key to the future of Etera, but how those pieces fit together, they would have to wait generations to understand.

※

The sun beat down on the rebel group that Straf'Tor had exiled from Kayerm. They had traveled far enough that Straf'Tor's escort had decided they would not be turning back and had let them go on alone. The group was tired and dirty from the trek. Though they had witnessed the Rah-hora as the other Mothoc had, from their experience so far with Laborn, who had taken over leadership of the group, the others knew better than to speak of it before he did.

Laborn spotted an outcropping of overhanging

rock in the distance and waved to the others before pointing ahead to their destination for the night. The group continued on until they were gathered under the protruding ledge.

Several of the males went in ahead to see if the cave was clear of inhabitants. Within a few moments, they came out and said it was safe to enter. Exhausted and glad to be settled for the evening, the females began gathering materials for resting places. The younger offling scattered to find kindling while the others looked for larger logs. Some of the sentries returned with gourds filled with water from a nearby stream and passed them around the weary travelers. Dried fruits and nuts were produced from carrying baskets. Though not needed for warmth, before long, a comforting fire was blazing. Once things had quieted down, Laborn spoke to the group.

"I know you are tired, and I will not keep you from your sleep for long. I propose that since our escorts have left us, we should send a few sentries out while the rest of us remain here. A few males will be able to cover more ground more quickly than we can as a group."

"What will they be looking for?" asked his mate, Shikrin.

"Preferably, they will find a branch of the vortex system and lead us to a suitable permanent home. It was a mistake settling at Kayerm; we need the rejuvenating power that a strong vortex provides. It may be a way off, but the more distance between Kayerm and us, the better."

"I saw a large patch of blackberry bushes as we were approaching," stated one of the males, Salus. "With the little stream nearby, I think we can remain here fairly comfortably for a while. Where there is water, there are also others who need to drink, so there should be some easy game."

A collective sigh went through the females, who were tired of the trip and wished to find a new home as soon as possible. Before long, everyone was bedded down for the evening, several of the males taking turns on watch—only because nerves were unraveling, and it gave the group a feeling of security to have them in place.

Over the next few days, the group made do and enjoyed the time of rest. Before long, one of the sentries returned, saying he had picked up a magnetic trail leading northwest and that the current had become stronger as he traveled it.

"Northwest is as good a direction as any. Let us wait for the others to return with their findings, and then we will decide," said Laborn. Laborn's mate brought him a longfish and a few golden-bellies, just caught by the females spearfishing in the stream nearby. He ripped one open quickly and eagerly ate until nothing was left.

"You did not give thanks for its sacrifice, mate," Shikrin mentioned.

"I will give thanks when we are settled. Until

then, I do not see a reason to be grateful, considering our current situation," he answered her.

"Do not let our troubles make you bitter."

Laborn picked a stray bone from his teeth and flicked it to the side, then licked the rest of the fish from his fingers, ignoring her remark.

The other sentries returned with no more promising reports, so the next day, the group packed up and headed northwest.

Teirac found Nox'Tor sitting down by the Great River and cleared his throat as he approached. The Leader turned to see who it was.

"Adik'Tar." Teirac had been warned by Wosot of Nox'Tor's touchiness about his title. "The sentries have returned, and they report that the rebels are far along in their exodus from Kayerm. There is no reason to believe they will return."

"Just as well, but place sentries as far out as possible to ensure they do not. Leave them there with enough supplies to last through the next two moon cycles and the means to provide for themselves thereafter if need be. Ask for volunteers; surely there are some unpaired males who will not mind the assignment."

"Yes. I will make sure they have what they need."

Nox'Tor nodded but did not answer.

Headed back to Kayerm to tell Wosot what he

had been instructed to do, Teirac passed Kyana coming in the opposite direction.

⁂

Kyana sat down on the soft loam next to her mate. "I wondered if I would find you here."

"I was just collecting my thoughts," he said, staring off into the distance.

"I know it has been hard on you, losing both your parents and then being saddled with the leadership of Kayerm." She looked over at him.

"I can handle it. Do not trouble yourself about me," he quipped sarcastically, not bothering to turn his head in her direction. Instead, with a thick stick, he dug holes in the soil in front of him.

Kyana closed her eyes at his stinging retort. "What has happened to you?" she braved. "Why are you so angry all of a sudden?"

He now snapped his head to face her. "Maybe I am angry, but I have every reason to be. My father is gone or dead. He barely warned me he was leaving and gave me no explanation of what he was going to do. And all over *her*."

"*Her*? You mean his mate, Ushca?" she asked, frowning.

"Yes, *her*. If it were not for her, my father would still be here. All I have left now is my mother," he said.

So this is why he is so angry? He blames Ushca for dying? It was not even rational.

"My mother, not Ushca, should have been at his side. Moc'Tor's decree that females would mate with only one male changed everything. E'ranale chose Moc'Tor, and then Ushca took my mother's place with Straf'Tor."

"I do not know what to say to help you. I am sorry," she said softly. "But how can you blame Ushca for being murdered? How is this her fault?"

"Why is everyone arguing with me? If you want to help me, find me another female. I need more sons. And I will do better by them than my father did by me, I assure you of that."

"You do not spend time with your existing sons as it is. And how are we going to explain to our offling about you taking a second mate?" she asked.

"You will find a way, I am sure. Now be off," he answered curtly.

Rebuked, Kyana rose silently and left, letting the tears roll down her cheeks unchecked.

Back at Kayerm, she sought out Pagara. "I must find a second female for my mate," she told the Healer.

"I see. So he has not changed his mind?"

"No; if anything, he seems even more insistent. He says he needs to produce more sons."

"I am sorry," said Pagara, and she placed a hand on Kyana's shoulder.

"And I somehow have to explain this to our offling. Do you have anyone in mind who would be suitable? Someone mild-mannered, hopefully, to offset the harshness I see in him now. I think I have learned the reason; he is bitter over his mother not being Straf'-Tor's First Choice. He believes if Ushca had not pursued his father, Straf'Tor would have stayed with Toniss, and none of this would have happened."

Pagara sighed. "That is not how it works. But he is not ready to hear that no amount of regret and bitterness will change the past.

"I can think of several females to consider if you want suggestions."

"Yes, please. Right now, I trust your judgment more than my own."

Pagara named the females she felt would be suitable. Kyana nodded at each name, thanked the Healer, and left to mull over how best to proceed.

Kyana worked long into the night doing needless chores—anything to delay going to their sleeping area. Finally, when the moon was high overhead, she crept in, moving carefully so as not to wake Nox'Tor. Slipping in next to him on the shared mat, she edged as far away as she could. She turned her back and faced the rock wall. Her thoughts drifted back to years ago when they were giddy with excitement at being paired. Then their joy at the birth of their son, Norland, and later, his brother and two sisters. The times they sneaked off to find new places for love-mating—in the soft glades, under the starry night canopy with the sound of peeper frogs in the spring background. The family time together. *How did we get here? What happened?* She had thought he loved her. Had it all just been a lie? Or had his love been so shallow that it was as easily cast off as picked up? Whatever bond they once had together, it seemed it had been broken.

By the next morning, Kyana had planned how to meet with each of the three females Pagara had suggested. She would not let on the purpose; it would take some time to determine who she would choose. She did not intend for those not chosen to realize what was going on, so she tried to spend time with them as casually as possible.

Kyana found the first one gathering bedding for the sleeping areas. Faeya was one of the smaller Mothoc females with a body covering that was almost black.

"Good morning," Kyana said as she approached. "Would you like some help?"

Faeya looked up to see the Leader's mate and smiled. "Why, yes, of course. And the company even more than that."

Kyana knelt down near her and started pulling up the soft brush and raking it into a pile with her hands.

"What brings you out here?" Faeya asked.

"Fresh air and a break from Kayerm's bland interior. I usually do not care for the heat, but the breeze and working in the shade makes it very comfortable."

The two females chatted for some time until Faeya said she had enough materials, and they rose together, scooped up the piles, and carted them back to Kayerm.

Over the next few days, Kyana sought out both Lorgil and Nasha and then spent a great deal of time considering her options. All in all, she preferred Nasha but was afraid the name was too similar to Ushca. Faeya was the sweetest, but could Kyana do this to her, knowing she would accept because she would see it as a great honor? Could Kyana subject Faeya to Nox'Tor's new, foul personality? That left Lorgil. What a terrible position Kyana was in, knowing that whoever she picked could most likely have a better life with someone else. Finally, of the three, Lorgil seemed the best match, more confident in herself, less likely to be shaken by NoxTor's oppressive personality.

That evening, when Nox'Tor came to their bed, he asked Kyana about her progress. "Have you found me a Second Choice?" he asked as he lay next to her.

"I believe I have. Lorgil."

"Did she say yes? Though I do not know how she could refuse; it is an honor to be paired to the Adik'Tar."

Kyana turned her face to hide her reaction. What

had happened to him? This was not who she had fallen in love with. "I have not asked her. I will tomorrow," she said and turned over with her back to him.

"We will have to explain this to our offling," she added.

"You will find a way, I am confident."

It was true; he expected her to tell them and would take no responsibility for it.

Kyana suppressed a shudder when she felt his hand running down her side and then snaking around to cup her between her legs, his signal for mating. For a moment, she wondered if she could just ignore it.

"What is the matter?" he asked crossly when he felt her stiffen at his touch.

"I am just tired, that is all," she lied.

"Then it is a good thing I will have a Second Choice if you are going to be too tired for mating," he said in a huff, and turning over brusquely, he ignored her for the rest of the night.

⟨҂⟩

When Kyana awoke in the morning, Nox'Tor had already left.

Dreading every moment of what she was about to do, she sought out Lorgil. "May I speak with you?"

Kyana motioned for them to walk away from the morning fire. "I do not know how to approach this, so I will just say it. Nox'Tor has requested to take a Second Choice. And I have selected you."

"I do not understand," Lorgil frowned. "Those are the old ways. When it became the female's choice of accepting only one male to mount her, the practice of taking a Second and Third Choice was abandoned."

"Nox'Tor is Adik'Tar now. He sees fit to make changes."

"It would not be my preference, but I do not see that I can refuse. Would I move in with you in your quarters?"

"We will arrange for another living space next to ours. No doubt he will split his time between you and me as he chooses."

Lorgil reached out and touched Kyana's arm. "I am sorry. This must be hard for you."

Lorgil's compassion moved Kyana, who smiled weakly. "I will be speaking with our offling, and then no doubt Nox'Tor will make an announcement. If you wish to tell your parents beforehand, that would be best."

Since Nox'Tor expected her to handle this herself, Kyana rounded up her offling. Her firstborn, Norland, who was fully grown, carried his youngest sister, and Kyana took them on a walk to her favorite berry-picking spot to find the late summer raspberries, now bursting with freshness.

Once they had eaten their fill, she gathered them around her. "I have something to tell you. As you know, your father is now Adik'Tar of Kayerm, and as Adik'-Tar, he has responsibilities that do not necessarily fall to other males. Though you have not grown up with this custom, your father is taking a second mate."

Being older and understanding more, Norland and his brother, Dotrat, who was only a few years younger, frowned at their mother.

"I thought, from our history, that was part of the problem that caused the anger of the Great Spirit and sent the contagion," said Norland.

"It was the indiscriminate and rampant mating of the females without their explicit consent, and the females being continuously seeded. The females had no choice. This is different because I have a say; it is I who selected the female who will be joining our pod," Kyana answered.

"But she will not just be joining our pod," Norland objected. Kyana knew he understood that this arrangement would not only be one of protection and provision; his father would be mating with this new female.

"Where will she live? Certainly not with us," Dotrat said. Sensing the tension, the younger daughter started to cry. Her older sister, Lai, picked her up to comfort her.

"We do not always get to choose what comes our way. Your father has decided this, and it is up to us to make the best of it. But no, to answer your question, she will have separate living quarters. Any offling she bears will live there with her. And I expect you to make an effort to welcome and accept her," she said.

"I will do as you ask, Mother. But I do not think this is right. What does Toniss think of this?" Dotrat asked, referring to his father's mother.

"I do not think she knows," Kyana replied. "Neither, I assume, does Trak."

Nor did she think it would make any difference. Nox'Tor cared nothing for Toniss's mate, so Trak would not have any influence.

"Who is it?" asked her daughter, Lai, still holding Somnil.

"Her name is Lorgil."

"Lorgil seems nice enough. I am glad you chose her," Lai answered.

Kyana turned her head and squeezed her eyes shut, shutting off the stinging tears.

Norland stepped closer and put his arms around her. "I am sorry, Mother. This cannot be easy on you, either."

She nodded and leaned her head against his shoulder. The others gathered close, having seen that despite her strong front, their mother had been hurt by their father's decision.

They stayed huddled together for another moment, and then Kyana said, "Come. Let us pick some more berries and take them back for Lorgil. That will make a nice welcoming gift for her, yes?"

She discreetly wiped the tears from her eyes and led them back to the berry patch to collect as many for Lorgil as they could carry.

As they walked home, Kyana saw Nox'Tor speaking with Wosot. She motioned for her sons and daughters to go on, and Nox'Tor stared at her as she approached.

"I have spoken with our offling. They know what is happening." And then, not being able to help herself, Kyana said, "But they asked if Toniss knows of it."

Nox'Tor openly glared at her.

"Why would I have consulted with Toniss?" he finally said. "She is not the Leader; she is not Kayerm's Adik'Tar, and the running of Kayerm is not her concern. I will call an assembly tomorrow, and Lorgil and I will be paired."

He turned to Wosot. "Prepare a living space a little way down from ours. Let Lorgil know of it so she can begin moving in. I want to be paired before tomorrow evening."

"If you have no need of me, I will be leaving," Kyana said and walked away to catch up with her offling.

When her mate came to their bed that night, she pretended to be asleep.

The next day, Nox'Tor did as he had said, and soon everyone was assembled around him as he once more stood in his father's customary place. Kyana and their offling stood at the back.

All eyes were upon him as he spoke.

"I have called you together to announce some changes. Since my father has left Kayerm to me, I have decided that some of our customs must change if we are to flourish. First of all, the A'Pozz plant, which was used by Ridg'Sor to poison my father's mate, Ushca, is no longer permitted here. Now that there is common knowledge of its properties, it is too dangerous to have around. Secondly, no longer will females be paired to only one male."

A loud murmur rose up from the crowd. One female after another exchanged glances, their expressions ranging from confusion to anger. Nox'Tor felt his heart pounding, and for a moment, he feared an uprising. He scanned the faces and startled when he found his mother, Toniss, scowling at him.

"Please, please. Quieten down," he said. "I know this is a return to the old ways, but our numbers are greatly reduced. We will not survive long if we do not increase our population. One harsh winter or serious food shortage, and we could lose many of us. If that happens, we will not be able to recoup our losses. To that end, I have asked my First Choice, Kyana, to select a Second Choice for me. She has selected Lorgil."

He motioned for Lorgil to step forward.

No one was listening any longer. The crowd was stirring, and Nox'Tor could see his mother coming up to speak with him. Lorgil had taken a few halting steps forward and then stopped as Toniss marched past her.

"Nox'Tor, what are you doing?" Toniss asked as she approached. "Have you learned nothing from the tragedy of our history?"

"Not now, Mother," he hissed. "You are embarrassing me."

"*You embarrass yourself, Nox.* Why did you not come to me with this idea? You are Adik'Tar now, but that does not mean you do not need the counsel of others. Surely Wosot does not approve of this. Wosot was one of your father's most trusted advisors. And I am confident by the look on Kyana's face that she does not, either. Only a fool makes such huge decisions on his own. You have not enough experience to be making wide, sweeping changes."

Nox'Tor felt his anger rising at being humiliated in front of everyone. "It has already been decided."

"Then undecide it," she snarled.

"It is too late; I cannot. I will lose their respect," he whispered to her.

"*You already have,*" she snapped. Then she turned and strode back to her mate's side.

Nox'Tor was grateful for the clamoring of the population; hopefully, as a result, few had witnessed the exchange with his mother. He took a deep breath and clenched his fists behind his back. Seeing Lorgil stopped halfway on her approach to him, he waved her forward.

"People of Kayerm," he had to shout to get their attention. "Quiet. Quieten down now. I realize this may feel like a shock. I am not ordering you all to comply at this time. But let the idea sit with you, and you will see the wisdom in it. And as your Leader, I will pave the way for this change."

He turned to Lorgil and reached his hand out to her.

"Do you choose me over all others?" he asked her.

Lorgil placed her hand over Nox'Tor's heart and said, I, Lorgil, daughter of the House of 'Nas, choose you over all others."

Then Nox'Tor placed his hand on Lorgil's head and said, "I Nox'Tor, son of the House of 'Tor, accept you as my Second Choice."

In the back of the crowd, Norland put a protective arm around his mother and looked at his siblings, shaking his head. "An awkward and rushed ceremony," he scoffed.

"Come," Kyana said. "We must go and welcome Lorgil. It is the least we can do for the pitiful pairing she just experienced," and she led them to the front, where Lorgil was standing.

When they reached the front, Kyana realized that the murmuring crowd had not dispersed. For her offling's sake and for Lorgil's, she turned to address them. "Thank you for coming and witnessing the pairing of your Adik'Tar and Lorgil, who is now his Second Choice. My offling and I welcome her to our family. Please enjoy the rest of your day."

Hopefully, they would take that as a cue to disband.

It worked. Talking still, they slowly started to move away. As Toniss was leaving with Trak, she caught Kyana's eye and slowly shook her head as if to say that she was sorry for her son's bad judgment.

That evening, alone in her sleeping area, Kyana cried herself to sleep as she tried to block the sounds echoing up from down the tunnel. Sounds of the male she had committed her life to so many decades before, the male she loved, whose offling she had born, voraciously claiming his Second Choice.

CHAPTER 3

Like it or not, Pan could not stay hidden in her quarters for long. After freshening up in the personal area, she instinctively left to find her mother. Then she stopped. *Mother is dead. What am I doing?* Her mother and father were both gone; she must now find her way by herself.

With the Mothoc Healers and Leaders having left, including Rohm'Mok, she felt at a loss about what to do next. She found herself walking aimlessly, and before she realized it, was standing in front of Kthama Minor. She looked up at the huge rock put in place by those helping her father.

Suddenly she became aware of movement over to her right. "Tyria!"

"I did not mean to startle you."

"What are you doing here?"

"I come here sometimes," explained the Healer.

"I feel drawn to this place, and I do not know why. I know we are not supposed to keep the past alive."

"I understand, though," said Pan. "Despite the efforts to cloak its history, this is still a mystical place. I do not think the Akassa pay it any mind, though. Perhaps it is now a sacred place for Healers and Guardians to gather," she joked lightly.

"Perhaps so. How are you doing, Pan?"

"I am adjusting. And you? Your offling is growing," Pan said as she glanced down at Tyria's expanding belly.

"Yes. I left Kayerm just in time. I did not want it known that Ridg'Sor had seeded me. Thank you for taking me in, for your father taking me in. Your sister Vel has been particularly attentive to my needs. And she told me Oragur has offered to help finish my Healer training."

"You are a blessing, and I am glad to hear that it seems you will be staying with us as our Healer. I know you have family elsewhere, but—" Pan sighed and added, "I feel a need to get back, though I do not know why. I am not sure what to do with myself, to be honest."

"Any time you want to talk, I am here," Tyria offered.

We could both use a friend, Pan thought. "Thank you. Stay as long as you wish, do not let my interruption cut short your time here." And she left Tyria to her solitude.

Over the next few days, Pan struggled, and as a result, spent a great deal of time alone. She felt called to return to the meadow where she and her father had engaged the Aezaiterian flow and the Order of Functions, but she ignored it. As she was hiding in her quarters, someone clacked the announcement stone outside.

"Come in," she called out.

"Forgive me," said Dochrohan, "But a messenger has come to let your brother know that they have several females for him to meet at the other communities. I thought you would want to know."

Pan nodded. "Thank you. When will he be leaving?"

"I believe shortly. He said he plans to be back by the High Council meeting."

He is not wasting any time, Pan thought bitterly. She wondered if he intended to leave Kthama and live at his mate's home. Surely, he would not abandon her altogether

"Where is he now?"

"He was in the Great Chamber a moment ago."

Pan went immediately to find Dak'Tor.

"I hear you are leaving for a few days?" she asked.

"Two of the other communities have females for me to meet. I am excited, Pan."

"What are your plans, Dak? Do you intend to

take over the leadership of Kthama? Do you even plan to return here after you are paired?"

"If the High Council members, in their wisdom, decide that for me to take up the mantle of leadership is the best choice for the High Rocks, then I will bow to their judgment," he said. "But I think Hatos'Mok made it clear that would not happen."

"What about your responsibility? You are the first son. The only son. It is your place to lead."

"An act of chance. You should have been a male and born first. I am not cut out for it, trust me. I know this about myself, even if you do not."

Pan shook her head. "No one truly knows their own strength until they are tested."

"Again, in all the time since it was formed, the High Council has never overturned a Leader's choice of successor. You know as well as I that they will not now, either."

Pan had to look away to compose herself. *He is right.* "How long will you be gone?"

"I do not know. As long as it takes. I am traveling up to the Deep Valley, then back down to the Little River. It will take some time."

"Just let me know when you return. I hope you find a few females you like, but remember, which one you pair with will be the High Council's decision."

The weeks passed, and before long, it was time for the High Council to meet. Pan had already sent word through the community of the High Rocks that the High Council was reconvening there, so there was plenty of time to prepare. A large meeting room had been prepared, as well as temporary living quarters for the travelers.

Pan looked at the 'Tor Leader's Staff, still in the same place her father had left it. She let out a huge sigh, then walked over and stood in front of it.

Finally, she reached out and wrapped her fingers around it. She closed her eyes. *Kah-Sol 'Rin.*

A moment passed. Pan realized she had been expecting to feel something when she finally grasped the sturdy wooden staff. Some type of supernatural anointing, perhaps. Instead, only sadness came over her. It was as if taking the staff in hand made her father's death just that much more real.

She picked it up, feeling its heft and balance. The thick wooden staff was taller than she was, with an obsidian base. Through the ages of their existence, only a few had ever carried it.

Pan sent up a heartfelt prayer. *Please, Great Spirit, grant me wisdom that I will prove worthy of this role my father has chosen for me.*

Pan slowly made her way from her quarters to the Great Chamber where the High Council was waiting.

As she entered at the back of the room, conversation dwindled, and everyone turned in her direction. What faced Pan was a polarization of builds and features. Those left of the original Leaders were pure Mothoc. But there were also those whom she considered to be full-blooded Akassa—those who were to become the Mothoc's partners in the leadership of their communities.

Pan was aware that most eyes were not on her but on the 'Tor Leader's Staff. She paused mid-way down and realized that the huge room was in absolute silence. *Are they waiting for me to lead the High Council as well?*

She took her place at the front. "As Leader, I thank everyone for journeying here."

The 'Tor staff in her hand made it clear she had accepted the leadership of the High Rocks.

"I would like to open the meeting with any reports you wish to share about your communities," she continued.

The Leaders' reports were much the same. Life was going ahead, and interestingly, the Akassa seemed less affected by what had happened than were the Mothoc.

When they were done, Pan spoke again. "Dak'Tor left on his way to the Deep Valley and the Little River in search of possible mates. Does anyone have news of this?"

Hatos'Mok spoke up. "He left the Deep Valley quite some time ago. We had several females for him to meet, and my mate, Deparia, attended to him."

"He was still at the Little River when I left," said Pnatl'Rar.

Pan nodded. "Thank you. The last time we all met, we spoke about the laws. I would like you to consider again the idea of forbidding Healers to pair and bear offling."

Frowns all around. "What would be the purpose, Guardian?" asked Tres'Sar from the Far High Hills.

"It should be obvious. We lost Lor Onida as a result of giving birth to her offling, Liru. My mother died from a complication of being seeded. While I would not say the loss of any one member is more important than another, the loss of a Healer is devastating to a community. Had Kthama had a Healer here at the time my mother first started having pain, perhaps she would not have died. Something could have been done earlier."

Oragur stood up to respond. "In some cases, what you say might be true. Had the cause of your mother's pain been identified earlier, it could perhaps have been resolved, but no Healer who has seen the problem your mother had has known any to survive. And it seems severe to forbid Healers to pair and have offling because of one situation. Besides, my daughter Krin has just been paired and is hopefully soon to be seeded. What would you suggest in her case?"

"It was just at the last full moon that you

announced she wished to be paired. When did the High Council select a mate for her?" she asked.

"They did not. We assumed that a Healer should have the same right as a Leader to select their own mate," Oragur said.

The others looked at Pan.

"That is not what was agreed to. *What is happening to us*? Are we going to splinter and make up our own rules and guidelines?"

In that moment, Pan knew that if someone did not intervene, if someone did not step up and take charge, all the progress her father had made in bringing cohesiveness to the people would turn to ashes.

She steeled herself. "As you can see, I have accepted my father's choice that I lead Kthama," she announced. "And as my father was the High Council Overseer, I ask to assume that position in his stead. I would suggest my brother, but it is clear by his absence that Dak'Tor has other goals in life than service to our people."

She regretted the bitterness in her words, but it was too late.

"Guardian, Leader of the High Rocks, *and* Overseer of the High Council?" asked Hatos'Mok. "Are you not trying to do too much?"

"It is not my preference. But it is clear to me that if my father's legacy is to continue, to bring our people peacefully into the future in an organized fashion, then someone has to step into his place. If no one else wishes to, I am willing to make that commitment."

Pan kept her eyes straight ahead, not daring to look at Rohm'Mok.

"I have no objection," said Tarris'Kahn. "If the Guardian later finds it is too much, we can make other arrangements."

"If you agree with this, please stand. Those who oppose, please remain seated," said Hatos'Mok. The majority stood.

"Alright, Pan— Overseer," he continued. "What else do you anticipate that the High Council needs to do to move us forward?"

"Just as we now discussed. Agreements are entered into, but memories fade. Surely there is someone among us, like Lor Onida, who can scribe ideas into some type of record keeping. Someone who helped with the Wall of Records? I would start with that person or group."

"The keeper of the records who helped Lor Onida was—is—Varos," said Tarris'Kahn.

"Please bring him to future meetings. He must work with us to record what we decide, so all remains cohesive," Pan answered. Perhaps Varos knew what had happened to the scrolls. Why had no one thought to ask him?

She spoke again. "I also suggest we need some common structure of leadership in each community. My mother was a great help to my father, and I know he also turned to Oragur for counsel. So my suggestion is that each community form an inner advisory consisting of the Leader, the Leader's mate, and the Healer. This will bring balance to the decision making, though ultimately it is still the Leader's responsibility to make decisions."

"Your father often said how much of a comfort and guide your mother was to him, but what if the relationship between the Adik'Tar and his First Choice is not so satisfactory? Having the Leader's mate in a position of influence may not always be wise," put in Hatos'Mok.

"Like it or not," Pan said, "the Leader's mate is already in a position of influence. My advice would be for the Leaders to choose their mates wisely. Perhaps officially recognizing their influence will ensure that kind of decision-making," she said.

The rest of the afternoon was spent discussing how to move forward according to the Rah-hora. When they were finished, it was time for evening meal.

⁂

Pan waited as everyone filed out, hoping to speak with Rohm'Mok. Hatos'Mok had left the room but then stopped to wait for his son.

"Go on, Father, please. I will be along shortly," Rohm'Mok said.

Hatos'Mok looked at them both for a moment before turning and leaving as his son had asked.

Rohm'Mok turned to Pan, "My father is pressuring me to take over leadership of the Deep Valley. I think the loss of your mother has made him consider whether he wishes to continue with the stress of leadership while his personal life takes second place. I have not told him about us yet. But I must tell him soon so he can start preparing my brother. I am ready to leave the Deep Valley and be your mate."

"I understand. And it has worked out well that you did not tell him yet. I am not ready right now; there is too much going on. We have had a fragile start with the High Council, and I cannot risk fracturing it by creating a fight between the High Rocks and the Deep Valley."

"You are talking about my father resenting you if I leave the Deep Valley to be your mate?"

"Yes."

"Pan, I do not have all the answers; I only know that I want to be with you. And if you want to be with me, we must work it out."

"I certainly want to be with you. Just give me a while longer."

Rohm'Mok looked around before taking her hand and pressing it to his lips. "As you wish. But please do not make me wait forever. You will outlive me as it is," he joked. "Now, I must catch up with my father. I will see you tomorrow."

Pan watched him leave, and his words went through her like a knife. Her memory flashed back to the day in the meadow with her father when he had slipped and said that, as a Guardian, she would outlive everyone she loved. Rohm'Mok was right. She would outlive him. By centuries. Everyone she loved would die before she did, even their offling—unless one was also a Guardian.

The council continued to meet over the next few days. Pan and Rohm'Mok found time to meet in secret, but each bit of time they shared alone only made it that much harder to part again.

Just as another session of the meeting was wrapping up, Dak'Tor returned from his trip. He entered the meeting room with a small, lighter-colored Mothoc female.

"You are back. Who is this with you, brother?" Pan asked.

"This is Ei'Tol," he said. She is from the Little River. I have chosen her as my mate."

Pan's jaw dropped, but, catching herself, she closed her mouth quickly.

"You have *chosen* her? The High Council is in charge of pairing. Or are you saying you have changed your mind and are here as the new Leader of the High Rocks and hence have the right to choose your own mate?"

"Was that decided? When was it decided that we could not choose our own mates?"

Exasperated, Pan turned away, clenching her teeth.

Hatos'Mok addressed Dak'Tor, "It was decided some time ago that only Leaders and the Guardian would be allowed to choose their own mates. But I do not believe you were part of those discussions."

"He may not have been present for that discussion, but at our last meeting, he asked to be paired." And Pan turned to face her brother again.

"You asked to be paired; you asked to travel to meet some potential mates from which the High Council would choose the best match. And now you appear with your own choice?"

Dak'Tor skimmed the room as if for help. Ei'Tol shifted on her feet and looked like she wanted to be anywhere but there right then.

"It was a misunderstanding," Dak'Tor said.

Tyria stood to speak. "This is what the Guardian has been trying to make us realize. We must find a way to record our decisions. Without a record, there will be a chance of *misunderstandings*. Distortions.

"However, considering the circumstances, my opinion is that we allow the pairing of Dak'Tor of the High Rocks and Ei'Tol of the Little River."

Pan glared at her brother. *A misunderstanding.*

"All in agreement, rise," she said irritably. A majority stood.

"Alright, as Overseer, I will pronounce you paired before the High Rocks after the evening meal."

Pan shot one last look at her brother and

dismissed the High Council meeting. She called Dochrohan over and asked him to make sure that any items Ei'Tol had brought with her were delivered to Dak'Tor's quarters.

That evening, when the Great Chamber was at its fullest, Pan walked to the front of the room to make the announcement.

"Though we are still adjusting to the loss of Moc'Tor and E'ranale, life must move forward. My brother, Dak'Tor, is taking Ei'Tol of the Little River as his mate."

She waited a moment for the chatter to die down and signed for Dak'Tor and Ei'Tol to come forward and stand on either side of her.

The same rhythmic chant rose from those present and echoed off the chamber walls. Then everyone fell silent, and placing her hands behind her brother and Ei'Tol, Pan drew them around to face each other.

She turned to Ei'Tol, "Do you choose Dak'Tor over all others?"

Ei'Tol placed her hand over Dak'Tor's heart and said, "I, Ei'Tol, daughter of the House of 'Dor, choose you over all others."

Then Pan turned to her brother and asked, "Do you accept Ei'Tol as your own, over all others?"

Dak'Tor laid his hand on Ei'Tol's head and said, "I Dak'Tor, son of the House of 'Tor, choose you over all others."

"May you enjoy long life together." At that, Pan could not help herself; her eyes raked the crowd to find Rohm'Mok.

Well-wishers came forward, and as quickly as she could, Pan excused herself and left the Great Chamber, hurrying to the solitude of her quarters. It did not take long before that solitude was broken.

At the clacking of the announcement stone, she practically ran to the doorway. "Rohm!"

She stopped short as she saw Tyria waiting for her. "Oh."

"I am sorry, Guardian. I— I should not have been so bold as to come to your personal quarters," and she swung around to leave.

"Wait, please," Pan stepped forward and reached out to the Healer. "Please do not leave. Please come in and talk to me. What is it you need?"

Tyria stepped inside haltingly and looked briefly around. Pan walked her over to a seating area with several large boulders, and they sat down.

"Why have you sought me out? Is something wrong?"

"Yes. Again, I am sorry for intruding."

"I am glad you are here. I need someone I can trust. I need a friend," Pan said softly.

Tyria reached out and touched Pan's hand, "You

can trust me, Guardian. I will do nothing to harm you, nor will I let harm come to you if I can help it.

"I want to say openly, yes, I am staying at Kthama. I know you made mention of it earlier, and I did not answer, but I have no desire to return to my own community. There was bitterness within my family when I left to follow Straf'Tor."

"Thank you; I am very glad you are staying." Then Pan covered her face with her hands as she tried to stop herself from breaking down. "I have made a terrible mistake, Healer. I have let myself become involved with Rohm'Mok from the Deep Valley. You heard me call out his name when I came to open the door," she said.

"It is not a mistake to love someone. Does he not care for you in return?"

"Yes, he does. I know he loves me as I love him. But I am torn because he wishes to be paired soon, as I did, but now is not the time for him to leave his home. As you know, I cannot leave Kthama, so Rohm'Mok would step aside, and his brother, Bahr'Mok, would take over as heir."

Tyria sighed. "You are worried about relations between the High Rocks and the Deep Valley."

"In part, yes.

"—But you came to my quarters to ask me something. Please, tell me what I can do for you?"

"Are you sure you do not want to talk about it? I know you must be so hurt by everything that's happened."

"No, please. There is nothing I can do about anything right now, and changing the subject will help. So, do tell me."

"I wanted to ask you please to reconsider forbidding Healers to pair and have offling. I understand that you have your reasons, but to prevent us from the greatest joys a female can know seems unfair."

Pan looked at Tyria for a few moments. "I will consider it because I trust you, and I know that I must have the counsel of others in order to make the wisest decisions. I will not mislead you; my feelings in this regard are strong. But I am glad you came by and that you spoke of this."

"Remember, your secret is safe with me. I will not betray you," Tyria said softly and stood to leave. "Get some rest. I do not mean to be unkind, but you look very tired. It is not normal for a Guardian to look so. Your father looked the same before he left us."

Pan watched the Healer leave and returned to her own thoughts. *Today I have found a friend.* She got up and walked over to the smooth polished portion of the wall to look at her reflection. Tyria was right; she was tired. She needed to engage the Aezaiterian flow, but that also meant the Order of Functions. Pan was not ready to submit to the Great Spirit. *Not yet. In the end, you will win, but for now, I hold myself back from you.* The Great Spirit had taken her father and mother, and she was not ready to forgive that.

CHAPTER 4

The members of the rebel band led by Laborn continued their journey to find a new home. Because one of the sentries had sensed an intensifying magnetic current to follow, they were no longer wandering aimlessly and made good time. In addition, they were mostly passing over level terrain. Laborn made sure they stopped to rest frequently. Some of the females were seeded, and they had a few elderly in their band, parents of some of the younger rebels, who had left with them not wishing to be separated from their offling, and one older female, Useaves, who was the closest to a Healer they had.

One evening around a late fire, Kaisak observed, "The current is growing stronger the farther we follow it. That is good news. My hope is that we find a suitable cave system near the wellspring."

"That would be a blessing—if I believed in such things any longer," Laborn answered.

Kaisak let the Leader's comment go. "With the rate at which the current is increasing, I believe we are close."

Several weeks passed, and then, off in the distance, they could see a large range of mountains. The greenish tint on the lower elevations promised trees, cover, wildlife, water sources. Laborn felt hope rise in his heart and immediately staved it off. Hope was for offling who needed protection from the truth of life's hardships.

As before, he ordered sentries ahead to scout out the area in closer detail. The rebels had gathered and hunted on the journey, but their stored supplies were nearly depleted, and they needed to set up a permanent location before cold weather. Even though it was easier on them with their heavily-haired bodies, time was running out.

Kaisak took three other males with him and went on ahead as Laborn had ordered. Running, and stopping only briefly, they reached the range by twilight. They had passed a decent-sized stream as they approached the rise, but they would wait to explore until dark when any night predators would have left their den. Then, the males would have time to explore without disturbing anything. With orders to call out if they found something promising, Kaisak sent Drall in one direction and the other two males another way while he took the straight-on approach.

They all scattered. Some time passed before Kaisak heard a whoot call. Both he and the other two sentries moved in the direction of the signal.

Drall stood in front of a fairly large opening that was nicely sheltered by a large overhang.

"What have you found?" asked Krac.

"Come and see for yourself. There are no inhabitants, from what I can tell."

The three entered the opening and looked around. Could they be this blessed, Kaisak wondered.

The ceiling of the entrance was not as high as Kayerm, but it was sufficient. The opening necked down a bit but on exploration opened into several branches a little way in. The four looked at each other.

"Split up, be back here shortly, though. And step heavily so you can follow your tracks back," Kaisak said.

"The vortex is strong here. Not as strong as the stories of what was below Kthama, if they were true, but still—" Drall said before they parted.

Time passed, and they eventually met up again.

Drall spoke first. "I saw no problems the way I went. The walls are solid; there is little moisture and plenty of other passageways. We can always carve out separate living spaces if there are not enough alcoves already."

"The tunnel I explored quickly took a sharp turn and then fell off to a very steep downhill grade," said

Krac. "It would not be safe to use; we would have to block it off."

"Easily done," said Kaisak. "There is more than enough rocky material here."

"The center branch goes deep," observed the fourth male, Org. "Plenty of opportunity there. Of course, it gets darker the deeper it goes, but we would not need to use all of it unless our numbers grow considerably."

"Let us return to the group," said Kaisak. "It will need further exploration, but it is warranted. At least there is hope for our people now."

Laborn was awake early and saw the sentries approaching. Kaisak waved, and theypicked up their pace.

"You are back sooner than I expected."

"Good news," said Kaisak. "We have found a promising cave system. Our initial exploration finds no issues that cannot be fixed."

"Fixed? Such as?"

Krac explained about the tunnel with the drop-off. Laborn nodded. "Any nearby water sources?"

"Yes," Kaisak answered, pleased with their finding. "A good-sized stream just before the incline starts. If it is still running this late in summer, I would say that it does not dry up. This is good news, is it not?"

"We will see," said Laborn. "As soon as we are able, you will lead us there. We will lodge outside overnight until we are confident it is safe to move in."

Laborn's males thoroughly investigated the cave system over the next few days. They immediately blocked off the dangerous tunnel, piling up as many large boulders as they could roll into place so no one could mistakenly use it and get hurt. When they declared it safe, the group was allowed to move in.

The females were happy with the nearby stream, and though the initial entrance was a little tight, the interior was dry and hospitable. Some went to the stream and set to fashioning enough spears for fishing. Efforts were underway to gather up food stores to winter over as well as carving out storage gourds and gathering bedding materials. Though the season was ending, several of the older offling set out to look for late-bearing berry bushes. Spirits were high; they were happier than they had expected to be and nearly everyone felt blessed to have found such a suitable new home.

At Kayerm, Kyana was still struggling to make peace with Nox'Tor's taking of a Second Choice. She tried to keep her spirits up, but most at Kayerm could see that it had hurt her deeply. Many of the other females worried that their mates would soon be asking for the same arrangement, and they began competitively eying the unpaired females.

Kyana had begun rising before first light to walk down to the Great River to take solace from the never-ending rush of water flowing by. She usually sat on the bank and splashed her feet in the shallows.

That particular morning, her solitude was broken when Pagara joined her unannounced.

Kyana turned when she heard footfalls swishing through the soft grass leading down to the river bank.

"Good morning, Healer," she turned to say.

"You are up early. Big plans?"

"No. I just like starting my day here," Kyana said, turning back to look at the water again. "I was wondering. Do you miss Tyria?"

"Yes. I miss her company, and I miss the reassurance of having another Healer here. Why do you ask?"

"My oldest daughter is interested in apprenticing with you if you feel she would be a good choice."

"I know Lai. Odd you should mention that, as I have for some time thought she had potential."

"Or perhaps not odd at all," Kyana suggested, and Pagara smiled.

"How is Norland doing?"

"He is angry with his father. I have tried to hide my feelings, but—" Kyana's voice trailed off.

"The other females are worried. And Toniss, she is still seething over what her son did. I do not think it is over between those two yet."

"It is as if something snapped in him. He is not the person I fell in love with. I wonder if I will ever get *him* back. If it were not forbidden now, and I could remember where it was, I think I would return home. There is nothing here for me any longer. Well, except my offling. But I would take them with me." Kyana sighed. "I do not know how to heal this wound, Healer. Have you any help for me?" Then she broke down.

Pagara leaned over and put her arms around the sobbing female.

On the hill, Kyana's oldest son was watching. Seeing his mother weeping into the Healer's arms, he turned and stormed down the hillside toward Kayerm.

Nox'Tor had just finished mating Lorgil and rolled off her. He lay on his back, panting, and Lorgil rose, saying she was going to clean herself up. As she left, Norland was heading down the passageway toward her.

"Where is my father?" he demanded.

"In my quarters. You may need to give him a moment—"

But Norland brushed past her. Not bothering to announce his arrival, he stormed into the room.

Nox'Tor sat up with a start and then jumped to his feet.

"What is the meaning of this, storming in here?" he demanded of his son.

"Mother is down by the Great River, crying. Are you aware of that? No, of course not, because all you see is what you want to and what suits you. You have hurt her terribly, and she did *nothing* to deserve it. How could you be so heartless? What has happened to you, Father?"

"Calm down. You are making too big a deal of this. Your mother is the one who selected Lorgil, so how can she have a problem with it? You are too young to understand."

"I am certainly not too young to understand, and I do not ever remember seeing Mother cry. I will never forgive you for this. You are supposed to protect the people who follow you, not use them for your own selfish purposes. You can hope that Lorgil bears you another son quickly because you have just lost this one." Norland turned and stormed out as robustly as he had entered. Lorgil was standing in the hallway, having stopped at hearing the commotion.

As Norland passed her, he said, "This is not your

fault. This is between my father and me. I do not blame you for this."

Lorgil cleaned up, but instead of returning to Nox'Tor, she went in search of Kyana. Eventually, she found her sitting on the river bank talking to Pagara and asked if she could join them.

She sat down next to Kyana. "Your son and Nox' just had strong words. Norland told Nox'Tor you were crying and how much he has hurt you by taking a Second Choice. I am so sorry to be any part of hurting you. I thought you were in agreement with it?"

Kyana shook her head. "Like you, I felt I had no position of strength from which to object. Now I wish I had, even though it would have created a rift between Nox'Tor and me. As it is, whatever was between us is gone; if I had my way, I would never share my bed with him again."

Realizing that Lorgil was not coming back, Nox'Tor stormed out to look for his son. Instead, he saw the three females huddled together down by the river. *This cannot be good.* In a moment of better discretion, he turned and left them to themselves.

At Kthama, the second summer heatwave had
passed, and the deciduous trees and bushes had
already turned and lost their leaves. In all the
communities everywhere, gathering and storing
efforts picked up. The Akassa females focused on
constructing and mending coverings for those who
wanted them—mostly the lighter-coated females,
who wore them for modesty, and occasionally the
elderly.

Months had passed. The High Council had once
again assembled. Pan scanned the group before
opening the meeting. To her dismay, there were no
Akassa in attendance.

Sitting in the back was Oragur with his daughter
Krin, who appeared to be seeded. Tyria was back
from her training with Oragur, also looking close to
delivering. Everywhere Pan looked, life was moving
forward—everyone's but hers. Next to Hatos'Mok sat
Rohm'Mok, and Pan dared not look at him lest her
feelings for him be obvious to his father.

Pan welcomed them and then opened the
meeting by asking if there were any announcements.
Oragur proudly announced that Krin was seeded,
even though it was obvious.

At one point, Pan pointed out that there were no
Akassa there and asked the Leaders why not. They
answered that the majority of the Akassa said they

were comfortable with Mothoc rule and did not feel qualified to question any decisions. Pan listened, for now saying nothing.

Pan then announced that Kthama needed a Healer's Helper. She asked the other Leaders and their Healers to consider anyone who would be suitable and willing to relocate to Kthama.

"Our Healer Tyria is obviously seeded. Once her offling is born, she will need the assistance of a Helper as the demands of motherhood will also draw on her time and reserves. Yes, we still have Tensil, but she is Akassa, and in some situations, she does not have the size or strength to treat us. Please bring anyone potentially suitable to the next meeting so Tyria and I can meet with him or her."

After the meeting ended, some clustered around Tyria and Krin, congratulating them. Pan, who had noticed Varos, the record keeper, took the opportunity to question him about Lor Onida's missing scroll.

"She did not give it to me, Guardian."

Pan felt that the disappointment on her face must be obvious. "Thank you, though."

She wanted very badly to escape to the sanctity of her quarters. She glanced over, and seeing Rohm'Mok staring at her, briefly shook her head as if to remind him that others might be watching.

Later that evening, Rohm'Mok came to her quarters.

Pan rushed into his arms, and he wrapped them tightly around her.

"I have missed you so," she said.

"And I have missed you. If we were paired, I would be here to comfort you through every hardship. There will never be anyone in my heart but you."

"Nor will there be anyone but you for me."

"Then I hope you will be able to forgive me," Rohm'Mok said softly.

"For what?" she asked, looking up with wide eyes.

"For this," he said, and he pressed his lips against hers and tightened his embrace around her, pulling her whole body tight up against him.

Pan stiffened for a moment but then relented and instead kissed him back passionately. Her longing for him surged and spread through her like wildfire. She could feel her self-control slipping. He was all that she could hold on to.

Deep within Pan, something broke. All her sadness and pain came rushing over her, and in that moment, all she knew was an overwhelming need to belong to someone, to have something stable in her life. She loved Rohm deeply. "I want you; I must be yours," she whispered into his ear.

"We are not paired," he whispered back, nuzzling her neck, his other hand caressing the back of her head.

"I do not care. Who knows what tomorrow may bring; we are here now and together, and I wish it never to end," she said.

Rohm'Mok hesitated, then whisked her up into his arms and carried her to her sleeping mat. In retrospect, he would have waited, taken more time with her. But the opportunity to become one was overweighing all other considerations.

He laid her down gently and then positioned himself over her, continuing to kiss her neck, her lips. He slipped one knee between her legs and then the other and leaned close, waiting at each movement for her to rebuke him.

"I need you," she whispered.

With a single motion, they were one, Rohm'Mok moving within her as she responded. Pan inhaled the musky scent of him, felt his warmth covering her. She drew comfort and assurance from his hard strength claiming her. She ran her hands down his back, feeling his solid muscles working to please them both. Time seemed to stop, lost up in the pleasure until finally, she stifled her cries as pleasure welled deep and blossomed to sweep through her body. His ecstasy mounted, and he emptied himself deep within her. The splendor given and received, Rohm rolled off and lay on the sleeping mat.

Within moments, Pan was filled with shame. What had they done? This was unheard of. No Mothoc mated another without a pairing, not since the time of her father's forbidding it. She had broken faith with her father and everything he sacrificed to save the Mothoc from themselves. *How can I be fit to lead if I cannot control my own desires?*

Rohm'Mok saw her pained expression. He rolled onto his side and pulled her to him. She buried her face in his arms.

"I am sorry, Pan. I am so sorry. This is all my fault. How could I let this happen?"

"No, it is as much my fault as yours. Oh, Rohm, what if I become seeded? My community needs me, and I have put at risk my entire credibility as Adik'Tar and as Guardian. My parents are gone, my brother will not lead. My sisters were never prepared in any way. The Akassa are shirking from the leadership. I am all Kthama has left to believe in. What have I done?" She did not want to break down, but she could not help it.

Rohm'Mok held Pan until her emotions had drained. When she finally quieted, he gently lifted her chin and looked into her eyes. "Say the word, Saraste', and we will be paired. I came here only to remind you again that I am ready to leave and come to stand at your side. Just say when."

It would solve a problem if I am seeded from this. But Pan could not commit to a day or time. She was not ready, and she had just proven that this was not the time for her to make life-changing decisions.

"Everything is in too much upheaval right now. Please understand; we have some time to decide when," she choked out.

Rohm'Mok squeezed his eyes shut. "Alright. We will speak of this again at the time of the next meeting. Perhaps that will give you the space you need to sort things out. I love you, and I want to spend the rest of my life with you. If you change your mind, I will live the rest of my life alone. There will never be anyone for me but you."

"Forgive me, but please go," she said softly.

Rohm'Mok then slowly stood up to leave. "I would never do anything to hurt you," he quietly said as he exited the room.

Pan rolled over, curled up, and lay on her mat for some time. She was failing. She was failing her father, and she was failing Kthama. She was failing herself; she was failing Rohm'Mok. Now she had to wait in agony to see if she was to bear his offling. Oh, please, let the cost of her weakness not be her peoples' faith in Etera's Guardian.

Weariness filled her body. She had not known such fatigue before. It was the need to enter the creative Aezaiterian flow. Eventually, she would have to. She could not avoid it forever.

Until the High Council ended and the group disbanded, Pan increased her resolve not to look at Rohm'Mok. Several times she caught Hatos'Mok eyeing her, and she looked away uncomfortably. *He suspects something.*

They had taken too many chances meeting alone. Perhaps someone had noticed and mentioned it to Hatos'Mok, or he had discovered it for himself. It was clear that she would not for much longer be able to avoid a final decision about Rohm'Mok and their pairing, whether she was seeded or not.

Weeks passed, and the signs Pan was waiting for, telling her that her beloved's seed had not taken root, did not come.

Tyria walked slowly to what had now become known as the Healer's Cove. The rest of the community had been advised to avoid the path leading in that direction. It provided a convenient way to prevent traffic, and it afforded Tyria the little privacy she had as Healer.

Winter snow had dusted everything, including the profusion of vines that covered the giant stone. Tyria cleared off a rock and sat down to seek counsel from the Great Mother; counsel for those she helped, those she loved, and for herself. She sat awhile after finishing her prayer and rubbed her belly, thinking about how soon her offling was due to be born.

As a Healer, Tyria knew there were herbs she could have taken that would have stopped the offling. But she could not do it, even though she had no mate to help her in raising him. Him. Was that a guess or a knowing, she wondered. She disagreed with Pan that Healers should not be allowed to be paired; the mantle became heavy at times. *And to deny us the greatest blessing of life, to have the love of a mate and the satisfaction of raising a family, seems unkind and unfair for what we give in return.* She would speak with the Guardian again before the High Council returned because she could feel Pan's determination to convince the other members of the wisdom in this radical point of view.

She also decided to consult with Oragur the next time he came to High Rocks. His own daughter, Krin, also a Healer, was paired and seeded. With him, she could perhaps build an allegiance and sway Pan's thoughts.

Back inside Kthama, Vel sought out her younger sister, finding her in the females cleansing area, an underground alcove where a tributary entered from above and passed through, eventually emptying out of the cave system. Pan was dangling her feet in the cold water, and Vel sat next to her.

"Greetings," said Pan, splashing her toes and sending little ripples out into the shallow pool, where they were quickly dissipated by the slowly passing current.

"Greetings, Guardian."

"Please; I get enough of that. I need no more worshipers, but I do need a sister. And a friend."

"Is that what it feels like?" Vel asked. "That some worship you?"

"Sometimes. From the Mothoc, I mostly feel respect. From the Akassa, it often feels like worship. We are so different from them; we forget how much. We are so much bigger and sense far more than they do."

Vel answered, "I do notice many of them step to the side as we come down the corridor. And when we eat, a form of segregation has sprung up on its own. Mothoc on one side, and the Akassa on another. Like it or not, a different division has come to our community."

"The Akassa Leaders have stopped coming to the High Council meetings. Do you think they fear us?" Pan asked, concern edging her voice.

"Not fear, "Vel said. "But we are like the mountains, a backdrop to their lives. We have always been here. We are part of their landscape. They are not to speak of the Wrak-Wavara, and that also shrouds us in mystery, makes us even more separate from them. So, fear us, no. They see us as their protectors, I imagine, more than anything.

"But I came to seek your advice. There is someone who wishes to be paired, but her family has recently suffered many losses and wounds. She does not want to add further to their troubles."

"A problem I can relate to, to be sure."

"What can I say to her to help her realize her happiness would not be a burden to them?"

"If you are asking how I would counsel her, I would remind her that depriving herself of the joys of life does not deplete the well of blessings from which others have the same right to drink. And if her family loves her, which I am sure they do, they would want her to be happy. Despite the burdens they bear, they would ultimately rejoice with her in choosing the direction in which her heart leads."

Vel sighed and sat quietly next to Pan.

"Now, tell me, how long have you wanted to be paired?"

"You knew I was speaking of myself?"

Pan chuckled. "I did not have to use my supernatural Guardian powers to figure it out either." She put her arm around Vel and drew her close.

"I have felt ready since before Mother became so sick. After that, it did not seem right to plan on anything with her condition."

"And then you did not wish to ask for fear of hurting me, seeing how I reacted to Dak's decision."

"I know you do not wish to be Kthama's Leader. I feel guilty having free choice to direct my life when it seems you have so little."

Pan shook her head. "Oh, sister, thank you for your compassion. But your life needs to move forward. Trust that things are unfolding as they should, even when the signs suggest otherwise."

"You sound like Father."

"I suppose I do. It feels good to have a sliver of faith return. I suggest that we put this before the

High Council when they next convene. Let that be the happy start to our next meeting. I will let you know so you can put your request before them yourself."

Vel hugged Pan tighter and then put her own toes in the pool, and the two sisters began splashing the waters together.

At the Deep Valley, the Healer Oragur, his mate Neilith, and his daughter Krin were preparing medicinals in the Healer's Quarters. "What is going on between Hatos'Mok and his son Rohm'Mok?" asked Neilith.

"I sense a great tension between them. I can hazard a guess that it has something to do with the Guardian," Oragur answered. "And it is not to do with High Council business."

It was not like her mate to gossip, so Neilith surmised it must be causing him a fair amount of concern. "Well, we agreed that something was building between Rohm'Mok and the Guardian when we were last at the High Rocks."

"It seems it has grown, but the problem is, the Guardian made it clear she would not leave Kthama to be paired. Any mate would have to move there."

"Hmmm," Neilith answered. "Hatos'Mok has spoken of handing over the leadership for a while now. If his heir left, it would fly in the face of his plans. Do you truly believe Rohm'Mok would do such a thing?"

"Males have made far more drastic choices for love than that. Look at Moc'Tor."

On the other side of the Deep Valley, Rohm'Mok absentmindedly walked the corridors, deep in thought. They had received no word from Pan, and he and others were to travel to Kthama soon. But the clouds forming above-ground threatened harsh weather. They could travel in shelter along the Mother Stream, but in the past, Hatos'Mok had been reluctant to leave Awenasa in times of bad weather.

Rohm'Mok felt a compelling need to spend time with Pan, to convince her to put herself first for a change so they could be paired. *And I still need to speak with my father, whether she is seeded or not.* Hatos'Mok would be angry and needed time to accept the new situation and prepare Bahr'Mok to take over as Leader.

As he was deep in thought, Rohm'Mok passed by his father, who put out a hand to stop him. "I would have a word with you."

"Yes, Father?"

"It is time to pass leadership on to you while I am still here to help you discover your strengths and shortcomings as a Leader. A wise Leader knows his weaknesses and when to rely on the judgment of others. This can only truly be learned once the mantle is accepted."

"Must it always be the first son to takes over?" Rohm'Mok asked. "At Kthama, it is not Dak'Tor who leads, but his sister."

"An uncommon turn of events, it is true, since Moc'Tor chose his daughter to lead in his son's stead. Dak'Tor was never very strong. His father and I were friends of a sort; I do not know if you realized that. He confided in me once that Dak'Tor coddled his own weaknesses instead of pushing himself to build on his strengths. Clearly, in the end, Moc'Tor doubted he would be able to overcome this short-coming and chose his daughter to lead instead."

Oragur approached as they were speaking, "I am sorry to interrupt. The sentries report that the clouds are gathering, the birds are alighting, and the other animals are bedding down—a serious storm front is coming. For our people's assurance, perhaps we should not leave at this time for a Council Meeting. And Krin is seeded, so I do not wish to leave her."

"What is your opinion?" Hatos'Mok asked his son.

"Putting myself in the Healer's position, I would not choose to be away either."

"Then, while the route is still clear, I will send a messenger to say we will not attend this time."

When Oragur had left, Hatos'Mok turned to his son. "What is behind your statement, your question whether it is always the first son who is chosen to lead? You are not willing to lead? But I have groomed you for this nearly your entire life."

"I am capable; you have said so yourself. But my heart is elsewhere."

Hatos'Mok eyes narrowed, and he set his jaw. "You do not want to lead Awenasa because your heart is elsewhere? Are you talking of a female? No, if it were a female, it would not be a problem. The females always come to the Leader's community. Unless—" Hatos'Mok leaned forward and locked eyes with his son, demanding the truth.

"It is true. It is the Guardian. We are in love and wish to be paired."

"*Bacht.* You are *in love.* What does that matter compared to the glory of leading the Deep Valley?"

Rohm'Mok stopped and stared at his father. "Do you not love Mother?"

"I love your mother, but my feelings for her do not drive my every decision. Love is a construct; it is a passing mood, enjoyable while it lasts. Pairing is to produce offling. If you choose wisely, the female you select will provide a path for your influence to reach into the future by giving you many healthy offling. And since the Akassa will not step up and lead themselves, you will have to be the next Leader here. But if you have any sense at all, you will realize that one female is fairly similar to another. Choose wisely, for a wrong choice can make your life krell. But keep it in perspective. A wise male does not give up his heritage as Adik'Tar for *love*."

"I thought you wanted to pass on the leadership so you could enjoy your remaining time with Mother."

"Oh, that," the Leader waved his hand. "It pleases females to hear such things. But the truth is, I am tired. I would like to watch someone else guide the community and bear up under these tumultuous times—without being in the middle of the storm. Besides, a new Leader should take over while there is still time to receive the counsel of his father to help him grow into his position.

"Now, put aside this nonsense of the Guardian and prepare to take your place. You will find a suitable female and one in whose shadow you will not always be standing."

Rohm'Mok glared at his father, seeing a callousness he had never known existed. Something did not seem right, almost as if his father was hiding something from him.

At the hesitation, Hatos'Mok scowled. "Come on, son. Do you really wish to be the consort of a Guardian? Please. And if being the Guardian were not enough, she is also Kthama's Leader *and* the High Council Overseer. Are you prepared to be satisfied with only the scraps of influence and admiration that fall from her table?"

"You are being disrespectful and unfair,"

Rohm'Mok practically snarled. "And my life does not rise and fall on the admiration of others."

"No. I am being honest and truthful. You just do not like hearing it."

"*I will be with her father*. You had best prepare Bahr'Mok to take over leadership of the Deep Valley. For I will not be here much longer."

Hatos'Mok whirled and slammed his fist into the wall, and small shards of stone flew off. "*Rok!* You cannot be serious. I could not have raised such a fool as this!"

Down the passage, others were gathering, hearing the commotion.

Suddenly, Deparia was coming toward them. "What is this?" she demanded to know, looking her mate and her oldest son up and down. "Everyone can hear you arguing. What is this about? I have never known you two to fight like this."

Hatos'Mok peered down at his mate. "Your son wishes to abandon his future right to lead Awenasa, for a *female*."

She turned to Rohm'Mok. "Is this true?"

"It is true. Father is upset that I have chosen a different path than the one he has decided for me. He refuses to acknowledge it is my right to direct my own life apart from his ambitions for me."

"And she cannot come here and stand by your side? I do not understand."

"The female he wishes to abandon his responsibilities for is the Guardian," Hatos'Mok snapped.

"Pan, daughter of Moc'Tor, who has responsibilities of her own as Leader of the High Rocks and Overseer of the High Council. Oh, and future mother of his offling. Apparently, that can be added to her list of responsibilities. She is not willing to shirk her commitments to be with him; however, she asks that he set aside his own."

Rohm'Mok took a step closer to his father. "That is unfair. She made it clear at the beginning that she could not leave Kthama."

In turn, Hatos'Mok stepped toward Rohm'Mok, and their faces were now very close together.

"You are right. She did. So *you* are at fault here. You pursued her, knowing that she would not leave her High Rocks. You went into this willingly, knowing the price of this union would be paid for by your people here. People who have grown up believing that you would in time step up to your responsibilities and become their Adik'Tar."

"Enough!" Deparia shouted and squeezed herself between the two giants. She put one hand on each chest and pushed them apart. They grudgingly surrendered to her will and stepped away from each other.

"I have heard enough of this." She turned to her mate, "I know you well. You are not a romantic. You are and always have been practical to the core. Never one to let your heart guide you."

She turned to her son. "And you. So unlike your father, you always followed your heart and expected your reason to somehow make peace with its decisions. You two could not be more different. It is no wonder neither can understand the other's position."

"Tell me. Do you love her?" she demanded of her son.

"I would rather die than not be with Pan."

She turned to her mate. "Like it or not, this is what will be. I should have seen this coming. I saw the signs back when the Guardian first came to the Deep Valley, but when nothing seemed to come of it, I dismissed it as my imagination.

"Rohm'Mok is of pairing age and old enough to make his own decisions. And no amount of your bullying or my objecting is going to make him change his mind. I suggest you get on to preparing Bahr'Mok and bury the future you had imagined. There is no battle here for you or me to win. All we will do is drive a wedge between ourselves and our son. A bitter wedge, which will only widen with time."

Hatos'Mok looked at his mate, so fiercely standing between him and Rohm'Mok.

"I leave you then," he stared at his son, "to the future of your own making." And Hatos'Mok stormed off.

Deparia turned to the crowd that had assembled, transfixed by the heated exchange.

"Please, leave us to work out our family matters in private. We are no different than you; we long for the same as you—to love and be loved. To belong. To find our place in the world."

The gathering slowly dispersed. Deparia and Rohm'Mok waited for the corridor to empty before they spoke.

"I am sorry, Mother."

"From the moment Pan came to the Deep Valley and I saw you two together, I noticed that look. As I have known from the beginning, your Father never felt that way about me, but I have seen that look on the faces of others. To find one's true and only mate is a sacred blessing and one that does not come to many. I certainly do not want you to leave home, but if that is how you feel about her, then do not let her slip from your hands, Rohm. No matter what the cost."

Rohm'Mok put his arms around Deparia, comforting her and taking comfort in return. "I need to go to her soon. Despite the foul weather, I believe she needs me now, more than ever."

Pan received the message with alarm. *The Deep Valley will not be attending the High Council meeting?* She would not see Rohm'Mok, but even more critically, Tyria's offling was due, and they had no other Mothoc Healer.

"Thank you for the message, Dochrohan. Is the messenger still here? If so, send a message directly back. Tyria is soon to deliver, and I need Oragur here." Her voice shook in spite of herself.

"The sentry is still here, Guardian. I will send your message back with him directly."

This could not happen again. No; never again. Despite there being no signs of trouble, Pan was adamant that Tyria should not deliver her offling without another Mothoc Healer there.

She sought Tyria out and found her resting in the Healer's Quarters. When she had been invited in, Pan tried to calm herself, not wishing to betray her alarm.

Tyria was not fooled. "What is wrong?"

"The Deep Valley sent a message that they do not wish to meet as planned due to potential bad weather."

Though the Mothoc were able to travel in virtually any weather conditions, the Leaders knew that in times of great strife, it comforted their communities to have them present. Anxiety and fear were not always logical, and during those times, the Leader would make a point of mingling with his people, letting them see his own confidence that all would be well.

"And you are concerned over my condition."

Pan nodded.

"Come and sit here." The Healer patted her sleeping mat. "I am fine, Pan. There are no signs of any trouble; I have no pain, I have no early contractions, I have gained a reasonable amount of weight.

There is no history of problems in my family line that any of us know of. My mother had no trouble delivering any of her offling, and like hers, my hips are widely set. Everything indicates that we will be fine. Tensil, the Akassa Healer, will be with me, and if it makes you feel better, we can have some Mothoc females available to follow her instructions."

"It is not enough. We need someone here in case something *does* go wrong." Pan shook her head and rubbed her face. "I asked for a Healer's Helper, and so far, one has not been identified. When we meet again, this must be a priority. In the meantime, I have sent a message to the Deep Valley, asking Oragur to come."

⚘

It was a few weeks later; the storm had come in and still not abated. Oragur had not come from the Deep Valley. Instead, Tensil was with Tyria, and several Mothoc females were also in attendance in case, for some reason, the Akassa Healer needed their strength.

Pan paced outside the Healer's Quarters until, finally, she heard the newborn's cry and let out a huge sigh.

Tensil opened the rock door. "You can see her now."

Pan hurried to Tyria, who was resting with her son cradled in her arms.

"Everything is fine, Pan, as I said it would be. Meet Fahr."

Pan looked into the offling's eyes and immediately knew that he would one day become a powerful Healer. *Another Mothoc Healer.* She gratefully looked over at Tensil, glad that there had not been any complications. The Akassa Healers had to rely more on education about the different uses of the herbs, flowers, roots, and barks than on the healing insight that came from the Mothoc connection with the Great Spirit.

She remembered her father's unfaltering faith— that despite appearances, things would unfold as they should. A pain of guilt flared at her neglect of the Aezaiteria and entering the Order of Functions.

Were they? Were events unfolding as they should? Or had her neglect of the Order of Functions allowed paths to be deflected from their intended directions?

Pan knew she must see Rohm'Mok somehow. She did not think she could continue to bear this alone.

CHAPTER 5

Toniss stood watching Nox'Tor and Lorgil as they strolled together down the path from Kayerm and disappeared around the bend, leaving deep tracks in the fresh white snow.

Having confirmed that they would not soon return, she sought out Kyana, who was in one of the back rooms lashing together a new hide curtain.

"May I join you?"

Kyana looked up to see Toniss and dismissed her daughters, who had been helping her.

"Please, yes," she said, beckoning.

Toniss sat next to Kyana on one of the seating stones. "My son has hurt you deeply. I see it. His Second Choice sees it. Everyone sees it but him. Or perhaps he sees it and does not care."

"I do not know if it is as you say—that he sees it but does not care. But at this point, I suspect that is true."

"Why do you stand by him?"

Kyana's eyebrows rose. "That seems to be a peculiar question coming from his own mother."

"Oh, I know I am too blunt. I have been accused of being cold-hearted. Perhaps it is true; I do not support my offling unconditionally. When I see they are failing, I offer a correction—and Nox'Tor has failed miserably in making this decision. I do not wish to add to your hurt, but I am not convinced it was made for the good of our people. The females do not wish to return to the old ways but now feel they must."

"You think he is that selfish, Toniss?"

"In the past, I would not have believed it possible. But he has let his father's disappearance harden his heart. In who he is now, I see little of the son Straf'Tor and I had together. Whether that hard shell can be broken, and he can return to his former self, I do not know."

"As for why I put up with it," Kyana answered, "I suppose it is out of respect for our community and for our offling. Everyone has suffered so much change, and change seems to be very hard for us. Though there is little left between your son and me, my station as his First Choice remains intact. I would be loath to deprive our offling of that foundation, even though my heart strongly wishes to do just that. But there is no place for me to go. And should I publicly reject him, to live here with further tension between us would only make matters worse."

"What is the new curtain for?"

"The opening to my living quarters. The last time Nox'Tor came to my bed and again found me sleeping, he finally realized I was intentionally refusing him. In his anger, he ripped the dividers apart and threw them on the floor. That was some time ago, and I am just getting around to replacing them."

Toniss got up to leave, her reason for seeking out Kyana satisfied. "Shall I send your daughters back in?" she asked.

"No, let them have their leisure time, but thank you. And thank you for talking to me. In the end, it seems it is from the counsel of other females that we draw our strength."

Toniss nodded, "It is true, is it not? We are fortunate to have such strong males to walk our paths with us and to provide for us. But in many cases, they do not seem to be able to help shoulder our emotional burdens."

Kyana returned to her living space and hung the new curtain. She gasped as Nox'Tor suddenly came into the room.

"Why are you here?" she asked, since they had little to do with each other any longer.

"It has been long enough," he said and walked over to the sleeping mat.

"What are you doing?" she asked as he seated himself.

"You are always asleep when I come to you at nighttime. You are not asleep now."

Kyana's eyes opened wide. "Nox—" she stammered.

"What is it now? Too cold? Too hot? *Too busy*?"

She found her voice. "I— I do not wish you to mount me."

"Now?"

"*Ever*."

"What? Never? You cannot be serious. Why not?" He jumped to his feet.

"You seem to be oblivious to how much your taking of a Second Choice has hurt me. You see only your own needs and wants and none of anyone else around you."

"You make me out to be some kind of selfish monster."

"Not a monster, but, yes, selfish," she said more quietly.

"You are wrong. Lorgil is happy with me. The problem is you, not her. If you will not bear me any more offling, then I will take a Third Choice, one I will choose myself. And you can spend every night of the rest of your life in here, alone in the dark," and he stormed out, whipping the new curtains aside as he passed through.

Kyana winced as he left but was relieved that in his anger, he had not destroyed her new curtains.

But what she would give for a nice solid stone wall instead of the flimsy hangings. And oh, how she wished she could also erect a stone wall around her heart so Nox'Tor could never hurt her again.

She sat on the sleeping mat where he had just been, and in the protective privacy of her solitude, Kyana prayed for strength.

The next morning, Nox'Tor announced he would be taking a Third Choice. Lorgil stood silently next to him, refusing to look out over the crowd. No one spoke or moved, all waiting stiffly to be dismissed. Lorgil started to leave, but Nox'Tor grabbed her arm to stop her.

"Let go, please. You are hurting me," she said as she winced from his grip. "Owwww," she cried out.

"Let her go."

Nox'Tor turned around to face his son, Norland, who was already a size larger than his father. The Leader released his grasp on Lorgil, who quickly stepped a distance away.

"This is none of your business, son. Move along."

"The mistreatment of any female is every male's business. And I am *no longer* your son. I thought I made that clear some time ago."

In the background, Toniss, her mate Trak, and Kyana were making their way over as quickly as possible. Wosot soon joined them, and the crowd, which had started to break apart, now stopped to watch the unfolding drama.

Trak stepped forward to stand next to Norland. "I do not know what has happened to you, but you are destroying our community. It is clear the females do not wish to return to the old ways, yet you have decided that is how it should be because it suits your needs."

"I do not care what you think, Trak. You are no one to me, just the male who *roks* my mother."

Toniss stepped forward and slapped her son hard across his face.

"How *dare* you," she snarled. "How *dare* you speak so. You have no concept of what it means to be the Adik'Tar, and I am beginning to wonder if you ever will. Norland would make a far better Leader than you. Or your own brothers, who you never speak to any longer. If you cared at all about our people, you would step aside and let one of them take your place."

Nox'Tor snarled but did not move against his mother. Under his breath, he said, "*They may be your sons by Trak, but they are not my brothers!*"

"Your mother is right," said Wosot. "You should step down. On the day after you became Leader, you assaulted me because I did not address you quickly enough as Adik'Tar. You broke Sacred Law, but I did not press it as you were clearly under a great deal of stress. But you then made wide-sweeping changes without consulting anyone else, and now you have acted aggressively toward a female. No male of honor, and certainly no Adik'Tar, conducts himself so."

Nox'Tor spat on the ground next to Wosot. "You are all jealous and badly mistaken if you think Norland could lead Kayerm better than I. Besides, Norland is not qualified to lead—as he himself says, *he is no longer my son.* Now get out of my sight and let there be no more talk of this. I am the Adik'Tar, and anyone speaking against me will be thrown out just as my father expelled Ridg'Sor's followers."

And throwing a piercing look in Kyana's direction, he stormed off.

Wosot, Norland, Trak, and Toniss stood watching him leave. Kyana and Lorgil came over to join them.

"Nox'Tor broke Sacred Law," Kyana said, her voice low. "Your grandmother is right," she added, looking at Norland. "You *should* lead Kayerm."

Norland stared at her, "You are not serious."

"I think she is," put in Trak, "and I agree with them both."

"So do I," said Wosot.

Norland shook his head. "I just cannot believe he has turned into this bully, but there has been enough turmoil and upheaval here. I will not agree to forcibly usurp his leadership. And despite how he is acting, he is still my father.

"If you wish me to take over leadership of Kayerm, you must convince him to step down willingly. If you can do that, then I will accept the mantle. But more division is the last thing we need."

"If anyone had a chance of reaching him, it would be you, Toniss," said Kyana. "But after how he just treated you, I am not sure even you can influence him any longer."

"Word about how he acted today will quickly spread," Toniss pointed out. "He may not be able to find another female willing to be his Third Choice."

"I do not know what has happened to him," mused Kyana. "And no matter what he has done, I do not wish him, or anyone, to suffer. Something has changed him, embittered him. I believe it is his belief that his father abandoned him. I know he blames Ushca for that."

"How can that be?" asked Toniss. "How can any of this be Ushca's fault?"

Kyana sighed. "He told me that after E'ranale chose Moc'Tor, and Ushca was released from her bond with him, Ushca pursued Straf'Tor. His father then abandoned you, Toniss, to be with her. He blames Ushca for luring his father away from you."

"That is not how it was at all. I must set this straight with him after he has had some time to cool off. If that is what is causing this bitterness, perhaps there is hope after all."

"Kyana," said Lorgil. "May I stay in your space tonight? I do not wish to be alone with Nox'Tor."

"Of course. I would enjoy the company. And our room is more than large enough for us females."

Kyana's sons had taken separate quarters some time ago.

"I will move my sleeping mat now."

"Wait up," said Wosot. "I will help you in case he has circled back and decides he does not like your plan."

That evening, the two females sat talking before Kyana's daughters came in for the night.

"I am seeded," said Lorgil. "I wanted you to be the first to know."

Kyana looked at her, "Are you glad?"

"In a way, yes. At least I will have my own offling to love and care for."

"Does he know?"

"Not yet. Later, when he calms down, I will tell him. It will be a while before I show."

Outside Kyana's room, Wosot laid stretched out in the hallway. He hoped his presence would give them some peace of mind, though Nox'Tor had not yet come looking for Lorgil as they had suspected he would. In fact, Nox'Tor did not return to Kayerm for several days.

The Leader had stormed off, leaving his mother and the others behind. Without looking back, he did not stop until he was quite a way from Kayerm and far out of sight. He followed the curve of the hillside, taking no mind of where he was going. He only knew he wanted to get as far away as possible.

After a while, calmed down, he came across a small opening along the foothills of the mountain range. It was a small cave of only one chamber that he had often sneaked away to as a young offling. Still not wanting to return to Kayerm, he gathered supplies and made a place for himself to spend the night. Alone, he lay there in the dark, listening to the coyotes yipping from the far ridges. He knew that in time hunger would drive him back to the community, but he vowed he would wait to go back until he could not stand it any longer.

In the end, it was not hunger or thirst that drove him back, but loneliness. Traveling through the dark of night, he returned to Kayerm, steeling himself for whatever was to come. He was relieved when he found no one outside, only the barest glimmer of the night fire's dying embers. He quietly slipped through the halls and gently pulled back the hide curtain of the room he shared with Lorgil. His heart sank when he saw their sleeping mat empty. Exhausted, he found a water gourd, and after quickly draining the contents, took his place alone on their sleeping mat.

From his position outside Kyana's living space, where he had faithfully remained since the altercation, Wosot saw Nox'Tor slinking away around a corner. Confident that the Leader could not get past him to the females and family inside, Wosot stretched out again and got as comfortable as he could for the remainder of the night.

※

Early the next morning, once Kyana and Lorgil had safely gone about their daily business, Wosot found Toniss and told her that Nox'Tor had returned and where to find him.

Hoping he would still be there, Toniss made her way down the passages.

Exhausted, Nox'Tor did not hear his mother enter but did wake when she crouched down next to his sleeping mat. Before he remembered where he was and what had happened, his face lit up at seeing her familiar face.

"Get up. I need to speak to you."

Nox'Tor sat up and pushed back to rest against the smooth rock wall. The events of the past few days came back to memory and his smile faded.

"I am going to speak now, and you are not to interrupt. Listen carefully to what I tell you, as your future and the wellbeing of Kayerm depend on your truly paying attention and not waiting for me to stop talking just so you may disagree. Nod if you understand."

Nox'Tor nodded; the last few days of living on his own had softened some of his steely arrogance.

"Centuries ago, long before you were born,

Moc'Tor took over leadership of Kthama from his father. Moc-Tor was revered by the community and held in high esteem by the other Leaders. He was a visionary, a true Leader. In those days, the males mated indiscriminately with the females. Though Moc'Tor was often approached and could have mated as many females as he wanted, he kept to his three. E'ranale, who was First Choice, and Ny'on and Ushca, who were his Second and Third Choices. As you know, in time, it became necessary for Moc'Tor to order that one female would be paired to one male, and that was it. Furthermore, it was the female's right to choose. Of course, this soon happened across all of our communities.

"Though Moc'Tor treated all of his females kindly, there was only one true love in his life, and that was E'ranale. So it is true what you have said, when E'ranale chose Moc'Tor, then his Second Choice, Ushca, was free to choose another male, as was his Third Choice, Ny'on."

Nox'Tor stirred to get more comfortable but wisely did not interrupt.

"E'ranale met with us females many, many times, trying to help us determine who to pick as our mates. We were uncertain, having been so accustomed to being used by the males at will without regard for our preferences. We had been taught that what we wanted did not matter. During the time before, your father mounted me often, though he also mated with other females. I do not know how many, but I know that there are several who bore his seed, and his offling are spread through the communities, as, no doubt, are Moc'Tor's. When we were discussing how to choose, E'ranale asked if I would choose Straf'Tor. Everyone was shocked when I said no, I would not choose Straf'Tor."

Nox'Tor sat up straight. "What?"

"Hush. I had the chance to choose your father. But it was I who rejected him. He did not reject me. It was a source of pride to be chosen by Straf'Tor, but our union was—uninspired—for lack of a better term. The truth was that Ushca and Straf'Tor had been in love for some time, but they denied themselves out of loyalty to Moc'Tor, Ushca being his Second Choice and Straf'Tor being his brother. Once the path was open for them to be together, they paired immediately, and from then on, they were inseparable."

Toniss paused to make sure Nox'Tor's attention was still with her.

"It is important you understand this. Your father did not cast me aside for Ushca. Nor did Ushca edge me out. I was not hurt by his pairing with her. I was relieved. Had it not been for this, I would never have been free to have the life I enjoy with Trak.

"So, if you are bitter because your father left, and you are blaming Ushca, thinking your father would have been with me if it were not for her interfering, you are dead wrong. If in your heart you must blame someone for this, it is me you should blame for never loving your father. But had I not stepped aside, your father and Ushca would never have been together. As a result, he would never have known true happiness. No one was hurt by what happened, except in your imagination."

Toniss paused for a moment to make sure Nox'Tor was still with her.

"So, tell me, now. Given the choice, would you prefer I had chosen your father though he was not in my heart and nor was I in his? Would you prefer your father had been denied the years of joy he found with Ushca? And that I could never have found happiness with Trak?"

Nox'Tor did not move. His eyes searched his mother's face. Finally, he slowly shook his head, no.

"It is important that you get your thinking straight because your misunderstanding is causing you great bitterness. Bitterness against Ushca, which is neither fair nor warranted. Your father loved Ushca; he never loved me. And I did not care because I never loved him either."

"It hurts to hear you say that," he said quietly.

"Sometimes, the truth does hurt. But it is only the truth that can set you free from your suffering. In this case, suffering based on a falsehood that you have decided upon in your own mind. Yes, your father lost Ushca, and with that, he lost the will to continue, but to love is to open yourself to loss. They are two wings on the same bird."

Nox'Tor waited to see if she was finished.

"I would like to be alone now," he said.

Toniss nodded and rose to her feet. She looked at her son a moment longer, praying to the Great Spirit that the truth would bring him healing.

❀

Nox'Tor sat there for a long time. It was not Ushca's fault. She had not taken his father away from Toniss. It did not change the fact that Straf'Tor had left, but if he and Ushca had loved each other as much as Toniss said, perhaps life without her was unbearable. *I used to love Kyana. But after my father abandoned me, I turned my heart against her.*

Though it was already daylight and he was very hungry, he stayed put, reflecting deeply on how he had behaved since taking over the leadership of Kayerm.

❀

When Toniss left Nox'Tor, she crossed paths with Wosot, who was standing just inside Kayerm's entrance. They locked gazes, and Toniss nodded slightly before going on her way. Wosot closed his eyes and prayed to the Great Spirit for healing for them all.

Nox'Tor left Lorgil's quarters sometime before high sun and gathered some supplies. Wishing to spend the day in solitude, he walked with his head down, not acknowledging anyone. He returned to the little cave he had found, to take refuge there once more.

***

That evening, Nox'Tor approached as Kyana and several others sat around the night fire. Toniss had told Kyana and Lorgil that she had spoken to her son, and asked them to pray that her words would take root in his heart and replace his bitterness with wisdom.

As he approached, Nox'Tor looked at Kyana with reawakened eyes. She was lit by the firelight, her beautiful dark eyes, her striking, almost black hair-covering—features which drew the eye of the other males—accentuated in the relief of light and darkness. He moved very slowly, making sure Kyana realized that he was coming to sit next to her. Out of the corner of his eye, he could see Wosot watching his every move.

Nox'Tor eased himself into position. He waited until she tentatively glanced at him and then held something out to her. She looked down, and he unfurled his fingers, revealing a beautiful red jasper stone. He took her hand with his other and placed the red gem in her open palm before curling her fingers around it.

Not wishing to break the sacred silence of the moment, he signed to her in Handspeak. "Maybe not today. Or tomorrow. Or the next day. Maybe not even this season. Or the next. But I pray that one day before I die, you find it in your heart to forgive me. I will do whatever it takes to win you back."

Nox'Tor rose as slowly as he had come and left the circle. The others stayed respectfully silent, having witnessed what they all collectively hoped was a step out of the turmoil and madness that seemed to have seized control of their community since Straf'Tor had left.

⌘

Lorgil entwined her arm with Kyana's. After everyone else had turned in, the two females sat together for some time, Kyana still clutching the red jasper in her hand. Tears stung her eyes. It was her favorite stone, signifying the love of the Great Spirit for everyone, as well as the individual love of one for another.

Finally, with the embers wicking out and the full moon high overhead, Kyana asked, "Will you stay with me again tonight?"

"Yes. As long as you wish. There is no happiness in the quarters I share with Nox'Tor."

Kyana nodded.

"Do you think he is sincere?" asked Lorgil.

"Time will tell."

"If he is, will you take him back?"

"I do not know. And if I do, what of you? It is far

less complicated with me out of the way. You can raise your offling together, and my life will go on as it has been these past months. I have become accustomed to answering to no one," said Kyana, a small smile coming to her lips.

"As he has been, he is no partner to me. I did not choose him, and there are no feelings between us; I am just a means to an end for him. It is different for you; your pairing was a result of the love that grew between you.

"Even if I could have prevented his seeding me, to escape being tied even more closely to him in life, I would not have. I understand you had to choose someone to be Second Choice. I do not resent your choosing me, for had you not, I would most likely not be bearing an offling now. In some ways, I think that is all I ever wanted, though it is harder to live without the help and protection of a male."

"I suppose," said Kyana quietly, "that until we both know if this reversal is genuine, we cannot see the next steps on the path. As for Norland, perhaps it is not yet time for him to lead Kthama. But he would make a great Adik'Tar, and though I wish Nox'Tor no ill will, I hope that one day the opportunity opens for Norland peacefully to take his father's place."

The females rose, carefully scuffed some dirt over the remaining coals, and made their way to Kyana's living quarters. Lorgil pulled her mat over closer to her friend's.

Settled down in the dark, Kyana said, "One good

thing that came out of this is that I have been given you as a friend. And for that, in spite of everything else, I am grateful."

Lorgil squeezed Kyana's hand, and they drifted off side by side, the red jasper tucked up safely against the wall.

(⚘)

Days passed. Nox'Tor gave everyone a wide berth, coming back to Kayerm only for supplies. Tensions subsided with his absence from the community.

Norland and Dotrat were entertaining their sisters outside in the deep snow. All were throwing wadded gobs of whiteness at each other, ducking, running, and laughing. Kyana sat watching them as she took a break from the daily chores of fetching fresh water, removing refuse, rationing food stores. Her youngest, Somnil, came running over to her.

"Come play with us, Mama. Join our side; Norland is winning!" Just as she said that, Norland came up behind her and swung her around in a circle, secure in his arms. She threw her head back with laughter, and joy filled Kyana's heart.

Hearing someone approach, she turned to see Wosot. "Looks like a happy family to me," he said.

She patted at the empty space beside her, inviting him to sit.

He joined her and sat quietly for a few moments, watching her offling romping together.

"May I speak plainly?" he asked, passing over a handful of dried grapes, which she happily accepted before nodding for him to continue.

"If Nox'Tor has truly repented and his transformation is real, will you take him back?"

Kyana squinted at Wosot. "I do not know. Forgive me, but the nature of your question surprises me."

"Because it is—so personal?" he asked, looking away into the far horizon.

"Yes."

"That is because I have a personal reason for asking it," he continued, plucking a stray blade of grass that peeked up through the snow and toying with it. He then shifted so they could see each other directly.

"The day you and Nox'Tor paired, the happy future I had been praying for was lost. I knew you had been seeing more and more of each other, but I thought there was still time. I was wrong. Time ran out."

Kyana frowned, and seeing the puzzled look on her face, he continued, "I waited too long to let my feelings for you be known. But I am asking you now if perhaps there is a chance for me. With you."

Kyana did not know what to say. He was protective of her and was helpful to her and her offling, but she had assumed it was only a product of his function in the community and his loyalty to Nox'Tor's father.

Sadness filled her heart as she thought of the

years during which he had held feelings for her and said nothing.

"It must have been hard for you," she said gently.

"Watching you with him? Watching your lives unfold together while I returned to my quarters alone night after night, trying not to think of you together? Seeing you seeded over and over? Wishing I was the one sharing your life with you, that it was me who had planted each offling within you?" He chuckled, but the sound was sad. "Yes, it was."

Then he looked at Kyana more intently than any male ever had. "But it is not your pity I seek. There were other females, others before Moc'Tor's ruling limiting us to pairing only, and there were also some who offered to pair with me. It was my choice to live as I did, and I have been resigned to it. But now, wondering if I could spend time with you and that perhaps you could learn to care for me in return, I had to speak my mind. I am not going to make the same mistake twice by keeping my silence."

For a moment, Kyana squeezed her eyes tightly shut, stopping the flow of tears at his heartfelt disclosure.

Wosot stood up, looking down at her. "Do not answer now. Take some time. In fact, you do not ever have to answer. If we never speak of this again, I will know your decision. But if you feel there might be a chance for you and me, please consider it. I know there is no provision for this, as you are paired with

him. But these are, above all, times of change." He
gazed off into the distance.

"I am not blind to the truth; I realize I am far
older than you deserve, but I could be a good partner
to you. A strong provider. And I would never hurt
you or put you second. Or ask to take another into
my bed. On that, you can rely." Having said his piece,
he glanced back at Kyana ever so briefly and walked
away as quietly as he had come.

Somnil saw Wosot leaving and came running
over. "Oh, join in. Please! Father doesn't play
with us."

The offling's words stabbed Kyana's heart.
Somnil is right. Nox'Tor never plays with them. He
never had.

In fact, now that she thought of it, almost everything her sons had learned about hunting, fixing,
banking a fire—all those skills were taught to them
by Wosot. Yes, Nox'Tor had spent time with them,
but it was Wosot who had taught her sons what they
needed to know as males. Only now did Kyana think
about how little time her mate had devoted to his
family. As for Wosot, she had never guessed that
everything Wosot did for them had come not from
duty but from genuine care.

Looking back at Kyana, Wosot shrugged and
joined in the fun. Soon he was on his back with
Somnil and her sister Lai flopping down on him and
her sons pretending to bury him with snow. Their
laughter warmed Kyana's heart. Even Norland,

already of pairing age, was joining in as if he had not a care in the world.

⁂

Later that day, Kyana sought out Toniss.

"What brings you to me?" the older female asked. "I heard that Nox'Tor wishes to make amends."

"Yes, though he is seldom around now. Perhaps he is giving me time to consider whether his turn-around is true or not."

"Do you want it to be?"

"I thought you would ask if I believed it was genuine, not whether I wanted it to be."

"Sometimes— Sometimes, no matter how genuine the apology, it is just too late. The heart has closed or moved on. Or the injury was so deep that even with forgiveness, the soul cannot re-open to the one who harmed it so deeply. I recognize that this is a possibility for you. At least, it would be for me if I were in your situation."

Kyana nodded. "I did not realize all these years how wise you are. You have been a big help to me, and I am grateful for that."

"Take your time. Move slowly. Small steps. A lot has happened, and your heart has been bandied about through all of it. I have nothing but the highest respect for you over your handling of the situation with Lorgil. How you have done everything possible to protect your offling from it, though despite your best efforts, they and everyone else here knows how deeply this has hurt you. No one will judge you, whatever your decision. Please rest assured that what I say is true."

"Thank you. You are kind as well as wise. I suppose I feared that if I did not take Nox'Tor back, you would turn away from me. And I would count that a great loss."

"Years have their way of teaching us—if we are willing to be taught. In matters of the heart, better a slow move than a wrong one." Then, in an uncharacteristic show of emotion, Toniss pulled Kyana over and hugged her as a mother would one of her precious offling. From that moment on, their relationship changed, and Toniss and Kyana were on their way to becoming friends as well as being relatives.

CHAPTER 6

Rohm'Mok took matters into his own hand, bade his mother farewell, and set out for Kthama. It was not long before a messenger brought word that he had arrived. Pan's heart sang and sank at the same time, knowing the message she had to give him would only make matters worse.

She walked into the Great Entrance, and as they were not alone, greeted him formally. "The High Council does not meet yet for a few weeks, though you are certainly welcome here. Let me find you suitable quarters; I assume you are staying for a bit?"

They walked together through the corridors of Kthama, Pan's mind returning to the time that seemed so long ago when, at the Deep Valley, she had first set eyes on Rohm'Mok.

She found an empty room, and he pushed the

stone door closed. As soon as they were alone, she fell into his arms.

"Why have you come? Though I am glad you are here, do not misunderstand me," she said.

"Too much time has passed, and I was not going to let a winter storm come between us. And I must tell you that I had it out with my father."

Pan looked up at him, waiting for him to continue.

"It went about as I expected, though my mother had to intercede on my behalf. As it stands, I am no longer in line to lead Awenasa."

"That was hard for you, I know."

"The worst part was learning that my father apparently never truly loved my mother. At least not as she loves him. He speaks of love as an option in pairing but not a necessity. And even worse, I discovered that my mother knows it to be true."

"I am sorry. For you and for her."

"I am here now, Saraste'. Please tell me you will not make me wait any longer?"

Pan let out a heavy sigh.

"Do not say it. Do not tell me again you are not ready. And could you be seeded? Do you know?"

Pan closed her eyes. *She could not put him off any longer. It was not fair to him, to their communities. Or to their offling.*

"I am seeded," she said.

He searched her face for meaning. "Are you happy? I cannot tell."

She smiled, "I am happy. I am not happy that I failed in managing my desire for you. But I am happy that I bear your offling. And I am very happy that you have come to me at this time. It will not be long before I show. Even now, it may be too late to pretend our offling was premature. But I pray that is not true, for I do not want my people to lose faith in me."

Rohm'Mok pulled her closer and wrapped his arms around her tightly. He leaned his head on hers.

"Will you stay until the High Council meeting? We can announce our pairing then."

"I can stay only a few days before I must return home. But yes, let us plan on announcing it then."

The weeks passed, and soon the High Council had gathered again. Once more, it was made up of only the Mothoc Leaders, as the Akassa preferred not to come. Rohm'Mok had returned ahead of his father.

As she had planned, Pan invited her sister Vel to announce that she wished to be paired. Then Tyria stood and told everyone that she had delivered a son, holding him as she spoke. The meeting was starting on a high note, and Pan was feeling joyful. Just as Hatos'Mok entered the chamber, she announced that she and Rohm'Mok were to be paired.

"So, it is official then? Nothing I said to you mattered?" he barked as he walked briskly to the front.

"What is the meaning of your disrespectful entrance?" asked Tres'Sar, rising from his seat.

"Did you not just hear? The Guardian and my son wish to be paired. He is abdicating his responsibility to the House of 'Mok and refusing to take over leadership of the Deep Valley."

Pan stood quietly, keeping an eye on Rohm'Mok.

The members of the crowd exchanged glances.

"Father, I have told you that Pan and I wish to be paired," Rohm'Mok said. "I do not see why you are still so angry."

"Please. It is not the wishing to be paired; it is your refusal to honor your responsibilities to your own community that is the disappointment."

Pratnl'Rar from the Little River stood. "This is a private issue. I do not see why it is being discussed in the High Council. Whatever problems this has caused between you, Hatos'Mok, and your son, are your family's business. The Guardian has a right to pair with whom she chooses. Though it is very unusual, your son has a right to refuse leadership of the Deep Valley. We who are Leaders, each with our own understanding of who will replace us when it is time to set the mantle aside, I know we can commiserate with your disappointment. But the cause for anger at the Guardian is unwarranted, and I find it highly disrespectful. Would you have talked to Moc'Tor so?"

"Thank you, Pratnl'Rar," said Pan gently, raising her hand. "But I can fight my own battles.

Hatos'Mok, if you wish to continue this conversation in private, I am willing to meet with you after this session has concluded. For now, we have other matters to discuss. Matters which affect all of us collectively, not just your house alone."

Hatos'Mok looked around the room. The looks on the others' faces made it apparent that the favor of the group was not with him. He sat down abruptly and waved for her to continue.

"As just announced, Tyria has had her offling. However, our situation here is not resolved. We have no Healer's Helper, and as Tyria's mate is not here, the burden on her as Healer and now as a mother will be considerable. Has anyone a suggestion for a Helper for the High Rocks?"

Pratnl'Rar of the Little River spoke up again. "I have someone who is interested. His name is Jhotin. I brought him with me for you and your Healer to meet. He is not here in the room, however, not being part of our council."

"Thank you. We will meet with you after we adjourn."

Suddenly, a cold rush of wind swept in around the stone door.

"This promises to be an exceptionally hard winter," Pan said. "Are there any special needs that we could help each other with?"

Tyria stood, still cuddling her son. "We have an abundance of Golden Seal this season. If any of you are lacking, I will be happy to share."

Dochrohan stood next, "We have more than enough Locust staffs if anyone is in need of them for winter spearfishing."

Pan smiled vaguely as the offers of help and sharing continued. She was brought back to the present by Tyria's voice.

"Pan," whispered Tyria. "They are asking you when you and Rohm'Mok are to be paired."

Pan looked at Rohm'Mok, who nodded slightly.

"Tomorrow morning perhaps, after first meal," she said.

In the back, Hatos'Mok glared at Pan, not even trying to hide his anger.

After some more discussion, Pan dismissed the group.

As everyone was leaving, her sister Inrion came up to her, "I am happy for you. Why did you not tell us?"

"I was struggling with the final decision."

"Because of your concern for Rohm'Mok?"

"Because of all my duties here," Pan said.

They stopped talking and turned as they heard voices rising from the back.

"Why would you come here and cause trouble like that?" Rohm'Mok was standing off against his father. "I thought we settled this back home, with Mother."

"You thought, because it was settled in your mind, and because your mother took your side, that was all there is to it? I want the High Council to realize what sacrifice the Guardian is asking of another—and for purely selfish reasons."

"I cannot believe you are talking of her like this. This is the Guardian. I never heard you challenge Moc'Tor as you are doing Pan. He managed to be Guardian, Leader of Kthama and Overseer, and he was paired and also had a family."

"Yes, but—" Hatos'Mok stopped.

"*But what?*"

Hatos'Mok glanced over at Pan, apparently only now realizing that she and her sister were still present.

"*Finish it.*" Rohm'Mok snarled.

When his father remained silent, he said, "You were about to say *this Guardian is a female.*"

Hatos'Mok narrowed his eyes and glared at his son.

"I do not know why this should surprise me," Rohm'Mok said, circling his father slowly.

"After what you said back home about my mother and the females' role. I did not realize this about you, Father. I am disappointed to learn you are shallow and narrow-minded."

Pan steeled herself to stay out of it. Had she not been the Guardian and merely the female involved, she might have intervened. But her position as Guardian carried too much authority, and this was not an official matter for her to resolve.

She turned to her sisters. "Let us leave these two to work it out. I doubt it will come to violence."

Vel and Inrion nodded, and they gave the two male giants one last look before leaving.

As they were walking, Vel asked, "Why did you not tell us that you had found someone?"

"Too much was happening at once. I met him when I traveled to the Far High Hills. He was not one of the males to be considered, but the attraction was mutual, and it just took us over. I do not know how else to describe it. I have tried to fight it, but I cannot."

"Nor should you," said Vel. "You have a right to happiness."

Back in the meeting room, tempers continued to flare. Rohm'Mok and his father still faced off, and others, who had stayed behind when father and son started exchanging words, were watching from a safe distance.

"What is it you want me to say, Father? I have made my decision. And nothing you can say is going to change it."

"This is not the time for you to leave the Deep Valley," Hatos'Mok said.

"If I leave that up to you, there will never be a time," Rohm'Mok answered.

"If you must pair with the Guardian, then I will give you my blessing. Only wait for a few weeks."

"For what?" Rohm'Mok asked. "What difference

will a few weeks make? Why the delay?" In a few weeks, Pan's seeding would be apparent.

"*Because your mother is dying, that is why.*"

Rohm'Mok felt as if the slightest of breezes could have knocked him over. "What? What are you talking about?"

"Your mother. She is ill. She has only a short time left."

"That is preposterous. A trick. She is fine; I just left her!"

"For the moment, she still appears fairly healthy. But she will quickly deteriorate. There is no question of it. It is not a trick. I speak the truth," said Hatos'Mok. "And before you ask, no; there is nothing that Oragur or any of the Healers can do for her. Her body is losing blood faster than its creative force can replenish it."

Rohm'Mok turned his back and closed his eyes. *This cannot be true. But this is too horrible even for my father to lie about. It must be true.*

He turned back, "How come I do not know of this? Why has Mother not told me?"

"Because she is your mother, that is why. She wished to spare you a long goodbye. She only gave me permission to tell you as we were about to leave. That is why I stayed back and only arrived now. Do not think poorly of her for this. She loves you and Bahr'Mok and only wants you to find your paths in life and be happy."

"Is this why you wanted to step down?"

"In part. Partly because of what I told you, that a new Leader should take over while there is still time for his father to help him grow into his position. But also partly because I knew her time was limited; I just did not realize I would lose her this soon."

"So you do love her."

"*Of course I love her*. I have always loved her. Not in the way that perhaps you love the Guardian. But the love I have for her has been enough. For both of us."

Rohm'Mok looked around the room, only now realizing that Pan had left.

"I do not know what to believe now, Father. The things you said back home about one female being the same as the next. Now, this. I do not know where the truth is any longer."

Hatos'Mok opened his mouth to speak.

"No," said Rohm'Mok. "I need time to clear my mind. I do not wish to talk to you again today," he said, and he briskly left the room.

Hatos'Mok watched his son walk away, and remorse began to fill his heart. He wished now that he had never agreed to Deparia's demand for secrecy. He would have said anything to try to convince his son to stay and lead the Deep Valley—for all their sakes. But now, he feared, he had gone too far.

Oh, Deparia.

What had he done now? Why had she sworn him to secrecy all this time? Hatos'Mok knew he would have said anything to convince Rohm'Mok to stay at the Deep Valley. For Deparia's sake—for all of them. But now— Now he feared he had gone too far. *My mate, you spoke of a breach between us, and I fear it has come.* For it seemed their son could no longer trust the words from his father's mouth.

When he was finally alone, Hatos'Mok found a place to sit and stayed in the room until dark shadows stretched across the rocky floor.

Rohm'Mok left his father and headed for the outside. Not caring in which direction he went, he took a path and followed it. Before long, he found himself at the cove which had been the mouth of Kthama Minor. He looked down to see a set of footprints in the snow and followed them.

Sitting alone on a rock, the snow lightly falling around her, was his beloved. He softly said her name, and Pan turned to look across at him.

He walked toward her, and brushing off a place on the rock, he sat down.

"How are matters between you and your father?" she asked.

"Better. Worse. I do not know. What are you doing here?"

"I come here to sit. Think. Reflect. Pray."

"The mystery still lingers here, does it not."

"How did it end between you and your father?"

"I still wish to be paired. Tomorrow morning. But then—"

Pan quietly waited for him to continue, holding the space for whatever he had to tell her next.

"After we are paired, I need to return to the Deep Valley for a while."

"How long?"

"I do not know. It is my mother. She is dying." He could feel the waves of grief coming off of him.

"Oh, my love! I am so sorry. Is there nothing to be done?"

"I do not know the details. I did not realize she was sick. My father has only just told me. Until a few days ago, she made him promise not to say anything."

Pan shook her head. "Yes, you should spend as much time with her as you can. Our pairing can wait."

"No. We must be paired before we part. I must know that I am yours, and you are mine. I can face anything if I am assured we will be together."

"You are assured of my love whether we are paired or not. But if that is your wish, then let us conduct the ceremony."

She stood up, pulled him to her, and held him for some time.

The next day, word was sent through Kthama that the Guardian and Rohm'Mok of the Deep Valley were to be paired.

Before the pairing ritual began, Pratnl'Rar of the Little River asked to meet with Pan and Tyria to introduce them to Jhotin, who explained his experience with healing practices.

Tyria questioned him on his knowledge of herbs, roots, and other medicinals. When she was satisfied with the extent of his knowledge, she asked, "Why would you consider coming here to Kthama? Do you not have family at the Little River?"

"Yes, I do; however, there is already a Helper there, and I know that this is my calling. I am willing to move to Kthama to follow it if you find me acceptable."

"Let us spend more time together before we decide on such a serious decision for both of us. If you can stay?"

"Of course. That is why I came with my Adik'Tar. Thank you."

Time permitting, as Tyria had to take care of Fahr, the two would spend as much time together as possible.

After the morning meal, the High Council and all of Kthama assembled in the Great Chamber. Rohm'Mok and Pan stood in front of the assembly.

The males were standing behind him and the females behind her. The rhythmic pairing chat began.

When it stopped, Pan faced Rohm'Mok, placed her hand on his heart, and said, "I, Pan, daughter of the House of 'Tor, choose you over all others."

Then Rohm'Mok placed his hand on her heart and said, "I, Rohm'Mok, son of the House of 'Mok, choose you over all others."

Everyone broke into smiles and came up to congratulate the couple. Hatos'Mok had settled at Rohm'Mok's promise to return to the Deep Valley for the short remainder of his mother's lifetime, and though he had watched from the back, he now also came up to congratulate them.

"I wish you hundreds of years of happiness together," Hatos'Mok told them.

"You can go home ahead of me; I will come tomorrow," Rohm'Mok reassured his father.

"Do not take too long," was all Hatos'Mok said.

Finally, they were alone in her quarters. Pan lifted her lips to his for their first paired kiss, and they took their time together, knowing they had a lifetime to share their lovemating. When they had finished, they lay together, this time without shame.

"Are you relieved we are paired," he asked. "Because of the offling?"

"I admit I am. But that was not a factor in the timing of our pairing, I promise you," she answered.

He drew Pan close and nestled her in against him with her head resting on his shoulder.

"I know that. Do you wish for a male or female offling?"

"I do not care. I only hope he or she is not a Guardian," she said sleepily.

"Because the coming of a new Guardian usually signals the death of the current one."

"No. Though I do not wish for a long life. You are what ties me to Etera. If it were not for you, I would be glad to join my father and mother in the Great Spirit."

Rohm'Mok squeezed her a little tighter and rested his head on hers.

"No," she continued. "I do not wish this burden on any soul. I wonder at the wisdom of the Great Spirit in choosing me for this; I am not my father, and I do not have his confidence, nor his conviction. I question everything. The truth of it is that I do not have his unwavering faith that things are unfolding as they should."

The moment she said that, a pang of guilt fell over her. The Order of Functions. *She had not entered either the Aezaiterian flow or the Order of Functions since her parents' death.*

"You only knew your father after he had gained centuries of life experience. You are young yet. It is not fair to compare yourself to him, both from that aspect and also because your path and what is expected of you are different from what was expected of him. You are too hard on yourself," he said softly.

"Perhaps things will look better in the morning," he continued. "It has been a difficult time. When I return from the Deep Valley, we will work to establish a routine, and I believe that will help settle things down for us both."

Pan did not say it aloud, but she wondered how long Rohm'Mok would be gone. She certainly did not wish for his mother to die, but she also longed to have him permanently at her side.

CHAPTER 7

Kyana spent her days going through the motions of raising her offling and trying to keep her mind off what was in her heart. She avoided Nox'Tor, who in turn seemed to have vowed to let her have her space. On several occasions, though, she caught him apparently studying Wosot.

Wosot also avoided Nox'Tor as much as he could, though his station did not give him much leeway in this. The tension between the two males was growing, and the community at large was feeling it.

Many nights at the evening fires, Nox'Tor would return and take a seat beside Kyana. They would sit together in silence until Nox'Tor finally left for the private quarters he had taken up at Kayerm. He was no longer welcome in either Lorgil's or Kyana's space, and his plans for a Third Choice had never come to fruition.

Occasionally, Kyana would turn in only to find a stone, shell, or a particularly colorful feather waiting for her on her sleeping mat. They were always very beautiful, and it softened her heart to think of him looking for these and leaving them to surprise her. She knew Nox'Tor was trying to make up to her, yet she struggled to open her heart to him again.

One afternoon, she approached Pagara and asked to speak with her.

After telling the Healer what she was going through, Kyana asked, "What would you do if you were in my position? Would you take him back into your heart?"

"I cannot answer that for you. Only you know the answer to that."

"It would be best for the community if I could find it in me to take him back to my bed. We have already been through so much. Perhaps I will try; the next time he sits next to me at the fire, I will speak to him."

Days passed with still no words between Kyana and Nox'Tor until the morning when he approached her as she was cleaning fish down at the Great River. The sun on her back was a welcome touch against the cold breeze coming across the waters.

"Good Morning," he said, startling her.

She looked up from her task.

"I will not bother you for long. I have come to tell you that I intend to invite Norland to the meetings I hold with Wosot and Teirac. It is time he was inducted into the leadership circle."

Kyana nodded. She washed her hands in the river and stood up, flicking off the excess water before turning to face her mate. "I am pleased to hear that. Perhaps, together, you can mend the rift between you."

She stooped over the carrying basket and arranged the fish she had caught.

As she straightened up, Kyana looked him briefly up and down. His hair was rumpled and his coat seemed unkempt. A pang of guilt ran through her, but she quickly pushed it down.

"Nox'Tor—"

"Lorgil keeps me from her bed," he interrupted her. "You have become friends; I want you to try and soften her heart toward me," he said.

Kyana's eyebrows shot up. "You want me to speak to the female you replaced me with," she asked, "and convince her to let you back into her bed?"

She could not help herself and threw the basket back to the ground.

"I did not replace you with her. You are still First Choice," he answered, his eyebrows pressed together.

"I need to go now." She leaned over and picked up the fish basket again. "If you want her back, you must find a way to win her yourself." What had happened to all his sincerity at the fire that night when he pledged he would win her back somehow? Now he was asking her to smooth things over between him and Lorgil?

"It is not fitting that there be dissent in our house, Kyana. I am the Adik'Tar. You need to respect that."

"You created the dissent. Not me. I do not know what you are thinking any longer. Or who you have become."

"It is Wosot," he said.

"What?" She stopped again.

"He is keeping you from me. I see how he looks at you. Is he pursuing you? You are paired to me and he has no right to look at you like that."

"Wosot has nothing to do with the problems between us. Leave him out of it." This time, Kyana brushed past Nox'Tor and walked off.

He followed her. "You are mine, Kyana; I suggest you remember that. If Lorgil will not have me in her bed, I will return to yours."

Kyana whirled around, "You are not welcome in my bed. *Ever*. Whatever was between us is over. I actually believed you that first night at the fire. When you said how sorry you were and that you would do whatever it took to win me back. And then the little gifts you have been leaving me, the pretty stones, the shells. I admit it touched my heart that you would go to so much trouble to gather them for me. But I can see that whatever caused you to say and do those things has since passed. Do not come to my quarters again. Ever. I am warning you."

"Warning me?" Nox'Tor laughed. "*Warning me?* What are you going to do, fight me off?"

"I cannot believe you said that. Are you saying you would force yourself on me? What about First Law, Never Without Consent? Not even the Adik'Tar has the right to set aside the Sacred Laws. Now you have gone too far!"

"What are you going to do—run to my mother again? Do not think I do not know that you have been talking together behind my back. That you have become friends!"

"Why should we not be friends? You do not control who my friends are. I am leaving now. Stay away from me; that is all I am going to say." And this time, she continued on despite his angry shouts for her to come back.

When Nox'Tor returned to his separate sleeping quarters, he found—lying on top of his sleeping mat—the red jasper stone he had given Kyana that night at the evening fire, along with a collection of shells, feathers, and other stones.

The next morning, Nox'Tor called an assembly. The people of Kayerm gathered around, wondering what was about to happen.

"I have decided that all unpaired males are to take a mate. You have until the next full moon to pick a female."

Toniss raised her voice, "It is the female's right to choose."

"Those times have passed. We are returning to the old ways because we need to increase our numbers. I have said this before."

Trak stepped forward. "And if they do not choose a female, what then?"

Nox'Tor glared at him. "Then they will never be allowed to mate."

"You cannot be serious?" someone asked, and the others started murmuring.

Nox'Tor looked at Teirac and Wosot. Out of duty, they stepped forward to stand by his side. Wosot kept his eyes off Kyana.

Toniss looked at Kyana and shook her head. Then she addressed her son. "You do not have the right to decide this."

"I do not? Who decided that I do not? I am the Adik'Tar. My father, Straf'Tor, and his brother, Moc'-Tor, changed the rules however they saw fit. Now I am making those decisions. I will not argue with you any longer.

"I suggest you males work it out among yourselves who gets who. And if there are not enough females to go around, you will have to share one."

Then he turned and walked down the hillside and onto a path that led away from Kayerm.

Pagara, Lorgil, and Kyana stood clustered together with Toniss and Trak.

"I never thought it would come to this," said Toniss. "Despite my best efforts, he is unable to let go of his anger at his father for leaving as he did."

"Do you think that is what is driving this? Is he trying to undo his father's ways as some type of revenge?" asked Kyana.

"That, but I think there must be other factors," Toniss said.

Kyana closed her eyes and let out a deep breath.

"If we let this continue, he will destroy our future," pointed out Trak. "We have an obligation to Etera to protect the remaining Mothoc blood. We cannot just arbitrarily start mating again. These decisions are not drawn from wisdom; they spring from a well of anger."

"We have no authority to challenge him. There is no provision for this," said Pagara.

"There is no provision for this; it is true. But if he can simply decide to change the rules, so can we," said Toniss. "First, he took a second mate, then threatened to take a third. Now he is forcing the females to accept a male not of their choosing. None of it seems to make sense."

"We cannot go through another upheaval," said Lorgil. "It has been nothing but that since we left the High Rocks. The rebel division took more of our numbers than we could spare, and we lost Tyria to Kthama. No doubt, the males are anxious to mate and will take this opportunity to follow his orders. They are under his direction."

"They are for now. But even their loyalty can falter if he continues in this vein," suggested Trak.

Kyana caught movement out of the corner of her eye and saw Wosot approaching the group.

"Come and join us," said Toniss. "What do you have to say?"

"My allegiance is to the Adik'Tar—according to the ways by which we have lived. However, I now question his thinking. I believe he is making these decisions for personal reasons rather than for the good of the community."

"Will the males comply?" asked Pagara.

"Some of them will," he answered. "Those who have waited long to be chosen by a female and have not been selected. But I do not anticipate happy relations under those circumstances. All this will do is create strife among us."

"We need him to step down and let Norland take over," said Toniss.

"Wosot, yesterday morning, Nox'Tor approached me about Norland joining your circle," Kyana said. "I believe he meant it as a peace offering to me—to begin letting him in on the leadership discussions. But I do not believe for a moment that he would consider stepping down."

"I do not see that we have a choice but to let this run for a while," said Trak. "Perhaps Nox'Tor's mind will clear and he will come to his senses when he sees the turmoil it is causing. After all, he is making decrees that he cannot truly enforce," said Trak.

"This is true. He cannot make the females accept a male."

At this, Kyana shook her head and looked away.

"What is it?" Toniss said. "Tell us. What has happened?"

Kyana did not want to answer, but they were all staring at her, waiting. "Nox'Tor demanded that I let him return to my bed. I told him no. He implied that it was not my choice," she told them.

Wosot's eyes feverishly searched Kyana's face. "He was saying he can force himself on you? *Without Your Consent?*"

"Where does Teirac stand on Nox'Tor's leadership?" Trak asked Wosot.

"I do not know. I will find out," As he spoke, Wosot did not take his eyes off Kyana.

Though the small group dispersed, Lorgil and Kyana remained standing together.

"Your offling is coming along?" asked Kyana, glancing down at Lorgil's mildly swollen belly. Only another female would have noticed it.

"Pagara says before the next summer's heat. So it will be a while. Nox'Tor no longer comes to my quarters, but after what you just said, I would be afraid to refuse him. I do not know what he is capable of—he might do something that could harm my offling."

"Did the news of your seeding not please him?" Kyana asked.

Lorgil looked down, "I have not told him."

"Why not?"

"I suppose I wanted the offling to myself a while longer. I do not relish being tied to him for the rest of my life. I pray it is not a male, as perhaps he will not be as interested in a female offling."

Kyana hooked her arm in Lorgil's. "Come. Let us take a walk. Soon enough, the refreshing snow will be gone. Let us talk of happier days and enjoy the relief from the summer heat while we can."

The two females walked arm-in-arm and talked together for some time.

Wosot found Teirac working with some of the other males to remove a tumble of rocks that was blocking one of the paths around Kayerm.

He drew Tierac aside. "About Nox'Tor's announcement. Where do you stand?"

"I did not know I had a choice. He is the Adik'Tar."

"For now."

"For now, and until he turns the leadership over to Norland? I do not see that happening any time soon if that is what you are implying."

"Will you choose a female then?"

"He has made it clear that I must. And the longer I wait, the less choice there will be. I suggest you do the same, Wosot."

Just then, Nox'Tor himself came up and interrupted them. "I see you are making progress on clearing the path," he said to Teirac while studying Wosot.

Then he added, "Wosot, considering your station, I think you should set an example for the others. I expect you to choose a female in the next several days. Choose wisely. I can assure you that a bad choice will only cause trouble for the rest of your days."

"I know what that is about," said Wosot.

"Do you? What is that about? Certainly nothing to do with you. This is not personal if that is what you are thinking," said Nox'Tor.

"And if I do not choose?"

"Then I will choose one for you. And I strongly suggest you do not let it come to that." Nox'Tor glared at Wosot. "You have three days."

The next few days were filled with tension and even outright bickering. A group of females found Toniss in her quarters speaking with Pagara. Toniss led them outside to a more private area.

"What are we to do?" one of them exclaimed. "We are being approached by males and told we must pair with them. We have no say-so? And some of the males have come to blows over us. There is chaos. Grunt said he chooses me, but I am repulsed by him. The thought of him touching me, mounting me—" A shudder passed through her. "Please tell us we do not have to comply? Tell us there is some way out of this."

"And there are more males than females," said another. "When he first took over, Nox'Tor said we would have to accept more than one male. Are they going to pass us around like property?"

"I do not know what might be coming," Toniss said. She thought for a moment. "Perhaps we need to meet with Nox'Tor together and confront him. He is creating a war between the males and the females, and our community cannot stand for it."

Early the next evening, the group of females, led by Pagara, found Nox'Tor speaking with a group of males, including Teirac and Wosot.

"May we have a word with you?" asked Pagara.

Nox'Tor peered around her at the assembly. Among them were Toniss, Kyana, and Lorgil. "What about?"

"We need you to hear us. We need you to listen. We are also part of this community, and we must have a voice in what happens to us."

"Perhaps from the others, but I did not expect this of you, Healer," he frowned. "You are part of the leadership. Your loyalty should be to me, not them," and he glared at the group with her.

"I am a female as well as the Healer. What you decide for them affects me too."

"Say what you have come to say then."

A few steps back, Teirac, Wosot, and the other males stood watching.

"We do not wish to be paired against our will. We know that the community has to grow, but there are reasons we have not chosen certain males as mates," she said.

"What possible reasons can there be?" he sneered. "You are the givers of life. It is your role to populate Etera. If you do not become seeded, there will be no more Mothoc blood entering Etera. Whatever your personal reasons are, they are not as important as your responsibility to the community."

Faeya spoke. "If we have to be paired, then at least let us choose. At least give us that," she pleaded.

Nox'Tor scoffed. "You have had more than enough time to choose. Years and years. I have made my decision, and I expect you to make the best of it. Now the males will get to choose."

He turned to Wosot. "Speaking of which," he said loudly.

Frowning, Wosot stepped forward with Teirac and the others following behind.

"Have you chosen yet?" Nox'Tor barked.

"With all due respect," Wosot said. "No."

The Leader's face contorted with rage. "Your time is up. As I warned you, if you are unable to choose, I will choose for you!"

He stormed into the group of females, who parted to make way for the abrupt intrusion. He grabbed Lorgil by the forearm and dragged her out.

"Here. Here is your new mate," he said and shoved Lorgil toward Wosot. She lost her balance and slid to the ground just in front of Wosot's feet. He bent down and helped her up before placing his hand across her as a shield.

"What?" gasped Lorgil. "But I am your Second Choice!"

"What are you doing?" Nox'Tor's mother, Toniss, stepped forward. "Are you out of your mind? Lorgil is your Second Choice."

"Well, now she can be Wosot's First Choice. She is not doing me any good. It has been long enough; she is obviously barren."

The females glanced disbelievingly at one another.

Kyana stepped forward to stand by Toniss. "This is not right. You cannot just set her aside like this, let alone force Wosot to take her."

"I will take the female," said Wosot.

Against her will, Kyana's hand flew to her mouth. Then she turned her back and choked back her tears. Her best friend, and— Oh, Nox'Tor was a monster. *He suspects something between Wosot and me, and he knows exactly what he is doing.*

"Take her then. Now!" Nox'Tor barked.

Wosot took Lorgil's hand, "Come with me," he whispered. "Do not worry."

As he led Lorgil away, he looked over to Kyana but could not catch her eye.

"See how easy that is?" Nox'Tor said to the males. "I suggest you all spend some time together and work it out. Time is wasting away, and I expect to be holding pairing rituals before too long," he glared at his mother and stomped off.

Pagara put her arm around Kyana's shoulder. "Please do not be upset. You know in your heart as well as I do that Wosot only did that to protect her. He will not touch her, but the next male might well have."

"Lorgil is seeded, Nox'Tor does not know," Kyana whispered through teary eyes.

Toniss turned to the males who had started to move closer to them. "I suggest you stop right where you are. These females are not yours to choose—that is their right. I do not care what my son says; you know he is wrong just as well as I do, only for some reason you are too afraid to stand up to him."

Teirac stepped out of the crowd of males, "He is the Adik'Tar. And he is your own son."

"He may be the Adik'Tar," she shouted, "but that does not give him the right to destroy everything his father and Moc'Tor struggled so to create. Do you think Straf'Tor would have wanted this? Would he support it if he were here? Do not let your blind allegiance block your ability to think for yourselves. We have come this far, and we cannot return to the old ways."

"He still holds the title," Teirac rebutted.

"He may hold the title. But by what means? Because he was the firstborn? He has not earned it," Toniss answered. "Nor has he proven he is worthy of it."

Kyana collected herself and joined Toniss. "Males, go on your way. You know what she says is right."

Neither of the females moved a muscle. Slowly the males dispersed, some grumbling, others looking as if they were considering what Toniss had said.

Finally, when all were out of sight, Toniss and Kyana turned back to the other females.

"What do we do now?" one of them asked.

"We find those who stand with us against Nox'-Tor," stated Toniss. "I did not want it to come to this, but it has. Nox'Tor can no longer be allowed to lead Kayerm. Each decision he makes is worse than the one before, and we must take a stand against him, but we need a sign to show us when that will be."

The females turned and slowly walked back to Kayerm.

Kyana hung back with Pagara and Toniss. "I have to go to Lorgil."

"Not yet," counseled Pagara. "You must let it be for a while. Nox'Tor will be expecting that—perhaps even wishing it—to give him another excuse to do who knows what."

Kyana balled her hands into fists and tried to steel herself for the days to come.

Wosot led a frightened Lorgil back to her quarters and helped her settle down on her sleeping mat.

"Do not worry, Lorgil. I will not touch you. Neither of us wants it, and I promise that you have nothing to fear from me."

"If you do not want this, then why did you agree to it?" she asked, still trembling.

"If I had refused, he would have given you to another male. And who knows what that male might have done." Wosot leaned over to catch her gaze. "You are safe with me. He has no authority to do what he did; you know that. I will watch over you, and in time things will right themselves. But for now, understand that no harm will come to you while you are in my care."

"Kyana."

"What about Kyana?" he asked.

"I have seen how she looks at you. And how you look at her."

"I understand. But for now, we must play this out."

Lorgil looked at Wosot and realized that she trusted him. That she always had. She remembered the nights he had stayed outside Kyana's quarters, protecting them both from Nox'Tor.

"There is something you should know," she said quietly. "I am seeded."

Wosot's eyes widened, and he could not help but

glance at her belly. "Ah. It is not yet obvious. How could Nox'Tor reject you for being barren when you are carrying his offling?"

"He does not know. I have not told him yet, though it will become apparent before too much longer."

"Who else knows of this?"

"Kyana. Pagara. Perhaps Toniss," she said. "I have not kept it from my friends. Only him."

"Is there anything you need for the night?"

Lorgil shook her head, no.

"Then rest now. I will sleep outside, and no one will get past me. Try to put all this out of your mind, at least for tonight."

<hr>

When Kyana went to her room, she saw Wosot leaning up against the rock wall at the entrance to Lorgil's, Their eyes met, and Kyana's heart pounded.

A long-drawn-out sigh escaped her lips as she entered her quarters. There she closed her eyes and said a silent prayer, *Oh Great Spirit. Please help me. I am lost and so confused.*

<hr>

After a day or so, Nox'Tor called another assembly. Had he been paying attention, he would have noticed that the single females and males were now separated, standing with a fair distance between them while the paired families clustered in the gap.

The community was once more divided.

Off to the side stood Toniss, Trak, Kyana, and Pagara. The younger of Kyana's offling stood assembled behind her, while Norland stood next to her, resting his arm around Kyana's shoulder. Wosot and Lorgil stood at a short distance from the others.

Nox'Tor addressed the males. "Time is passing, and I must know who among you has chosen a female."

The males glanced at each other, but no one spoke.

"Surely, some of you have made a selection. Speak up!" he demanded.

When no one answered, he turned abruptly to Teirac. "Explain! Explain to me how none of the males have selected a female?"

"The females refuse," said Teirac. "They object to your decision, and they will not comply."

Nox'Tor gritted his teeth, and his fists clenched. "What do you mean *they will not comply*?"

He swung around to face the other males. "I have given you a choice, and you refuse to take advantage of my generosity? Very well. You still have until the full moon. If you have not chosen by then, I will choose for you as I did for Wosot."

Wosot stood motionless, with Lorgil standing next to him.

"Wosot is now with Lorgil. They will be paired at

the full moon with the rest of you once you have come to your senses. We need to get on with it. We are wasting precious time."

"Lorgil is your Second Choice. How can she be paired with Wosot?" Finally, one of the males had found a voice.

"She is no longer my Second Choice. She has not produced an heir, so I have no use for her. My purpose in taking a second female was for offling. Since she has failed in that regard, she is now with Wosot."

Heads shook, and a murmur rose. "That is not right," said Ser'Hun. "You cannot just set a female aside like that. Nor can you *give* her to another male without her consent."

"Are you going to cause trouble for *me* now, Ser'Hun? Did my father's whipping, which left you crippled, not teach you a lesson about rebellion? You are lucky he let you live. I might not be so inclined."

Ser'Hun stepped back, looking to Toniss and Trak for help.

Toniss took a step forward, but Trak reached out and clasped her arm to hold her back. "No," he whispered. "Give it some more time."

Norland whispered to his mother, "What is going on? What is he saying about Wosot and Lorgil?"

"I will explain later," she whispered back.

But it was too late; Nox'Tor had seen them. "More dissension? And from my own family?" He marched over to Kyana and Norland.

"I was about to bring you into the leadership circle," he hissed at his firstborn. "But I can see that was a mistake. One of many I have made."

He then turned to Kyana, looming over her with his face only inches from hers. "Do you support me? I am asking you to tell me where you stand. Are you with me or against me?"

"No! I do not support you in this." She raised her voice, shouting right into his face as she let her anger fly. "It is ludicrous. You are not a law unto yourself; you cannot just take a female and then set her aside when your mood changes. If your father could see what you are doing, he would be ashamed."

"So you are also against me? Well, you are wrong. I am the Adik'Tar, and I can set a female aside if I choose to. In fact, I will demonstrate my authority to do so right now. You, Kyana, are no longer my First Choice. You are now free for any other male to choose you."

"This is preposterous!" Toniss stepped forward, unable to hold back any longer. "You have lost your mind, Nox'Tor," she called out as she marched closer.

"*Kal-Sol 'Rin!*" he shouted. "It is done. I will choose a new female." He turned and looked at Pagara.

Pagara took a step backward, putting up a palm and shaking her head, no.

"You," and he pointed at Pagara, advancing toward her. "You and I will be paired at the same time as the others. I suggest you prepare yourself and pray that you are not barren like Lorgil nor insolent like Kyana."

By now, the crowd seemed on the verge of a riot.

Teirac, who until now had been convinced that Nox'Tor was fit to lead, finally had his eyes opened. "You may be the Adik'Tar, but you have overstepped your bounds," he said. "I did not want to see it, but it is true. Whatever has happened to change you, you are not fit to lead."

He turned to the crowd, "Who agrees with me? Who else can see that Nox'Tor is not fit to be Adik'Tar?"

Nox'Tor stood, nostrils' flaring, as he watched thick fur-covered hands lifted skyward, no vote withheld.

"You see," said Toniss. "The Adik'Tar is powerless without the consent of the people. Without a following, it is only a title. You have no authority here any longer."

Toniss turned to address the crowd. "By our rules, the Leader must be of the 'Tor line. I suggest that Norland, first son of Nox'Tor, become Adik'Tar in his father's stead. How many are with me?"

Heads nodded, and voices agreed loudly.

Toniss turned to Nox'Tor and proclaimed, "*Kah-Sol 'Rin.*"

Nox'Tor's face contorted, and he lunged at his mother. He didn't realize that Trak and Wosot had moved closer to him when the shouting started. They jerked him back.

They held him as he struggled and glared at Toniss. "How could you? My own mother!"

"I may be your mother, but I also carry the honor of the Mothoc blood. We are the last hope of Etera. It hurts me deeply to see it come to this, but the needs of the community have to come before one person who is so in the wrong. We cannot survive under your tyranny. But if you think it gives me any pleasure to see what has become of you, you are dead wrong," and she turned away from him.

"You cannot do this! *You do not have the right.*"

"You gave us the right," Wosot bellowed, tightening his grip on the struggling male. "When you established anarchy. When you threw out the old ways. The laws are for all of us. If they do not bind you, they do not bind us. When you dispensed with the laws, you opened the way for this."

"What are you going to do with me?" Nox'Tor snarled.

"Do with you?" asked Wosot. "We are not going to do anything with you. You will live here with the rest of us. But you are no longer in command. No one will follow your orders. Your son will now be Adik'-Tar. Make peace with your fate, as it has been brought down upon you by your own hand."

Finally, Nox'Tor stopped struggling, and Wosot and Trak loosened their grip. He shrugged them off and stepped back from them.

"This is a mistake. You will see in time," Nox'Tor said, pointing at them as he backed away. He took one last look at the crowd, turned, and stormed off.

Kyana stood transfixed. *What just happened? Am I free of Nox'Tor? Is my oldest son now Adik'Tar?* She pulled her daughters to her and wrapped her arms protectively around them. Her other son, Dotrat, remained close by.

"Norland is now Adik'Tar," stated Dotrat.

The girls looked up at their mother, waiting for her to speak.

"Yes. Yes, he is," she said quietly.

"Is Father no longer our father now?" asked Somnil. Kyana crouched down to their level.

"No, Father is still your father. But he is no longer my mate. And he is no longer Leader; it was too much of a burden for him. We must pray that he finds peace now. We must all pray for him, understand?" The girls nodded.

Toniss, Trak, and Pagara joined her, followed by Wosot and Lorgil. Kyana was afraid to look at Wosot for fear he would read her mind.

"What do we do now?" asked Lorgil.

"Live our lives, move forward. Things will settle down." Kyana looked at Lorgil as she answered, her eyes begging a question.

Wosot answered, "I will accept Lorgil under my

protection until such time as she chooses a new mate."

"What does that mean?" Kyana could not help but ask.

"I will hunt for her and contribute to her wellbeing. That is all. It is difficult for a female with offling and no connection to a male."

"So you will not be paired," said Toniss.

"Lorgil does not wish to be paired with me," replied Wosot, now staring directly at Kyana. "Nor do I wish to be paired with her," he added. Kyana could no longer avoid his gaze, and her breath caught as their eyes met.

"I will help Wosot in return with gathering, mending, and tool-making," said Lorgil. "With his generosity in providing for me, I have no need of a male. I will have my offling and no mate to answer to, which is all I ever wanted."

"You may change your mind in time," counseled Pagara. "You are still young, but I can see this arrangement is suitable for you both."

Then she looked at Kyana and added, "For now."

"Lorgil, if you wish to move in with me, I would welcome the company," said Kyana, tearing her eyes away from Wosot's. "My space is generous, and there is more than enough room for you and your offling. I know my daughters will welcome you."

"I would love that. Wosot, would you help us?" Lorgil asked.

Wosot nodded, and they made their way back to Kayerm.

As they walked to Lorgil's quarters, she turned back to look at Wosot. "Once I move in with Kyana, why not take my quarters? They are just a short way down from hers. And you would not have to sleep outside the door."

Kyana let herself look at Wosot. "It would be more practical; it cannot be comfortable on that cold rock floor. Now that Norland will be Leader, he will not mind if you wish to switch living spaces."

"As you wish. As soon as you are settled in, Lorgil, I will take your quarters, then."

It seemed that a great burden had miraculously lifted, and the females smiled and chattered lightheartedly as Kyana and Wosot helped Lorgil move her few belongings.

Once Lorgil was settled in, Kyana invited Wosot to share the evening meal with them. Afterward, they all went out to the fire and joined those of the community already there. The others watched as the three came over and sat down. Before long, Pagara joined them. The smell of the fire was welcoming, and its gentle glow that bathed the circle created a feeling of community and intimacy among those there.

"You are free now," Pagara said to Kyana.

"I never expected that to happen. I do not even know if under our laws he has the authority to set our pairing aside, but I accept it," she admitted.

"It does not matter. Everyone heard it. No one would expect you to stay shackled to someone who would treat you like that."

"Has anyone seen him since the meeting?" asked Lorgil.

"I have been told he left for a while but has since returned and gone into his quarters," Wosot answered, "Do not worry, I will be vigilant."

After the confrontation ended, Nox'Tor had angrily headed for the little cave where he had found refuge earlier. Over time, his emotions quieted, and he was able to think more clearly. He had always had too much of a temper and he had let it get the best of him. Now he had no female, and had probably scared any others away. *What have I done?*

Maybe in time, Lorgil or Kyana would forgive him, and one of them would return. But he had seen the way Wosot looked at Kyana, and she at him. He knew that casting her off was the stupidest thing he could have done.

Tired of the small, cold hideaway and picking a time when few would be around, he slunk back to Kayerm and into his own quarters.

CHAPTER 8

Rohm'Mok returned to the Deep Valley to be greeted by Deparia and Bahr'Mok. As he gently embraced his mother, he searched her face for signs of illness.

"I can see it in your face. Your father told you that I am ill," she shook her head and stepped back. "Forgive me for not letting him tell you earlier. There was nothing you could do. Please give me good news that you and the Guardian have been paired?"

"Yes, Mother, he did. The Guardian and I have been paired," he answered.

"Then why are you here?"

"I need to be here with you." He looked at his brother for support.

"Your life is at the High Rocks now. You should be with your mate, at her side, not wandering around here waiting for me to die."

"Stop. Please do not talk so. Pan and I are in agreement that my place is here with you."

"Well, then I am going to have to hurry up and die then," she said, smiling.

"Please, I asked you, do not joke like that," Rohm'Mok answered.

"I am not afraid of returning to the Great Spirit; I have had a good life. I do not wish to suffer, of course, but death does not frighten me."

Deparia hooked her arm through her son's as a moist blast of cold air came in, blowing flurries of snow about. "Come, let us get out of this drafty entrance and sit down and talk. Oragur has said I should stay warm."

When the three of them had found a sheltered place to sit, Bahr'Mok spoke first. "I am glad you have returned, brother. Father told me that you will not accept the leadership. And we know the Akassa Leader, Lair'Mok, will refuse to take over. It is the same in all the communities; the Akassa feel it would be disrespectful to set us aside. So it will fall to me. I want you to know I respect your decision, and I welcome the leadership of the Deep Valley."

Rohm'Mok leaned over and placed a hand on his brother's shoulder. "I am pleased to hear this. You will make a fine Leader."

"Your brother and I have talked at length about it," Deparia said. "Your father's anger at your not accepting what he felt was your obligation was not a reflection on Bahr'Mok's leadership abilities. Your brother will make a fine Leader. And I can move on, knowing that both of my sons are happy with the paths they have found."

"Since you have lived with the idea of being Adik'Tar longer than I have," said Bahr'Mok to his brother, "I would be glad for any wisdom you have gained over the years while expecting to take over."

"I will be glad to help you. But Father has the experience, and no doubt he will begin training you —if he has not already. Besides, all the time Father was talking to me about leadership, you were the one asking the questions. You probably already know more about running the Deep Valley than I do!"

Rohm'Mok studied the way his mother was sitting. Now that he was paying attention, he could see a bit of a slump in her posture, more lines on her face than he remembered. Her body covering had lost some of its shine. He scooted closer and drew her over to lean on him.

"I love you, Mother," he said quietly.

She patted his hand. "I know you do, and I pray that you and Pan will have a long and joyous union and produce many offling."

Rohm'Mok wanted so much to tell her that Pan was already seeded, but he held his tongue. *I hope she lives long enough for me to be able to tell her.*

The three sat talking for some time until Deparia said she needed to rest. The brothers walked with her back to her quarters, where they waited for her to get settled before leaving.

When they were out of earshot, Rohm'Mok asked his brother, "How long have you known about this?"

"Do not be angry with me. I wanted to tell you, but she forbade it. She was afraid that if you knew, you would set aside your feelings for the Guardian and return."

"That should have been my decision to make," Rohm'Mok replied. "Do not judge her harshly. She wants more for you than she had with our father. She wants you to have the love she never had. I am not saying Father does not love her. But not like you love Pan."

Rohm'Mok sighed and leaned his head in his hands. "Where is Father now?" he finally asked.

"He was off talking to the Healer the last I saw him."

"I will see you at evening meal; I am going to find him."

⁂

He found his father in the Healer's Quarters with Oragur.

"How much time does she have?" Rohm'Mok asked, dispensing with niceties.

Oragur put down a bowl containing herbs he had been crushing. "Not long. It is good you have returned."

Rohm'Mok glared at his father. "I am glad I did not wait too long."

"Your father is ready to cede the leadership to you. Your mother would no doubt like to witness that before she passes. I would not delay," the Healer said.

"I am not taking over the Deep Valley. Bahr'Mok is. I have been paired with the Guardian and am returning to the High Rocks after my mother's passing. Bahr'Mok will take over instead."

Oragur looked questioningly at Hatos'Mok.

"I had hoped my son would have come to his senses, but as you can see, he has not. And Bahr'Mok has spent no time in training. So the transition will have to wait."

"You are just saying that to make me feel guilty," Rohm'Mok said. "You could hand over the leadership to Bahr and still be at his side to counsel him. It is not uncommon. Do not rob Mother of this happiness in an effort to control me. Pan and I are paired, and I will be returning to Kthama to serve the Great Spirit at her side. Nothing is going to change that."

Oragur spoke. "I have served as your Healer for several years now, Hatos'Mok. I have earned the right to speak frankly to you. Listen to your son. Set aside your stubbornness in this regard, and do not cheat Deparia of this last bit of pleasure. I assure you that if you do, you will regret it the rest of your days."

"What difference does it make if she sees the 'Mok leadership change hands?" Hatos'Mok raised his voice. "What can it matter? She is dying, and nothing will change that."

"Deparia deserves to see that her sons' lives will continue down a path she can visualize," said Oragur. "No doubt hearing that Rohm'Mok has been paired with the Guardian has pleased her. I know she wanted that for him. Now she needs to see Bahr'Mok finding his place too," said the Healer.

"By the Great Spirit," Rohm'Mok blurted out. "You do not want to pass the 'Mok staff to my brother because you still hope I will relent and take over here. Because once it is passed to my brother, it cannot be undone. You have heard nothing of what I have said. *You saw me paired with Pan. I will not be leading the Deep Valley. I will never hold the Leader's Staff!*"

"It is you who is being selfish. The Deep Valley needs you, *not* your brother!"

"It is my life. I have a right to decide its path. Bahr'Mok will lead just as well as I would have. *Better*. If you knew anything about us at all, you would realize that. But you have been so set on getting your own way that you do not even see who he is. He is far more suited than I am."

"What makes him the better choice?" Hatos'Mok shouted. "Give me one reason."

"Because *he wants it*. Whereas I do not! And if you had any idea who either of us is, you would have known that!"

Rohm'Mok paced a few steps and turned back to his father, "How many times did you and I go on long walks together that he asked to join in? We talked about the practicalities of ruling the Deep Valley, and it was he who asked the insightful questions. It was he who instinctively knew the best course of action when you tested us with imaginary scenarios. He was the one hanging on your every word. He has wanted this all his life, whereas *I never have*."

"Wanting to lead and being the best choice to lead are not the same," his father said.

"I know that. But in this case, it is true. He is just as smart as I am. And his heart is here. Mine is not. And never will be," Rohm'Mok said in a quieter voice.

Oragur stood watching silently. Finally, he spoke, "Your son is wise, Adik'Tar. Perhaps wiser than his father."

"Tell Bahr'Mok not to be late to evening meal," was all Hatos'Mok said before he turned and left.

Rohm'Mok glanced at the Healer. "Does that mean he hears me?"

"I would take that as a yes. Be patient with him; ever since you were born, he has expected you to take over."

"And my mother. There is truly no hope for her?" Rohm'Mok asked, his voice low.

"No, there is no hope."

Mealtime found Deparia with her mate and her sons seated at their customary table. One of the females had brought food over to Deparia, as her weakening state was now known to everyone. Bahr'Mok watched as she struggled to eat even a small amount. He looked over at Rohm'Mok seated on the other side of her, his face creased with concern. Her strength was waning quickly, and they had both realized it would not be long before she could not join them in the common eating area.

They ate quietly, all aware of Deparia's struggle.

Finally, when much of her food was gone, Hatos'Mok spoke. "It is time for you to take over leadership of Awenasa," he said as he pushed what was left of his food around in front of him. The others silently waited, unsure of to whom he was speaking.

Then he lifted his head and looked directly at Bahr'Mok. Deparia let out a long sigh, and a smile crossed her lips.

"You will make a fine Leader, son," she said to Bahr'Mok and reached her hand across the table to take his.

"Thank you, Mother," he said, trying to steel himself against the flood of grief filling him at seeing how weak she was.

"And you will do well in your role at the Guardian's side," Hatos'Mok said to his other son. "A Leader needs a strong helpmate. I have no doubt you will be a great asset to her in that regard. But no matter how busy and demanding life becomes, always make time for each other. Do not let anything come between you. As long as you have that bond, together you can weather any storm."

He glanced quickly at his mate. "I suggest tomorrow, after last meal, we have the ceremony for the transition of leadership."

"Do I look that bad?" Deparia smiled as she asked.

"I keep asking you please not to joke about it," said Rohm'Mok, taking her other hand.

"You have always been so serious. We all return to the Great Spirit at some point. My body will be discarded, but I will live on. As will my love for both of you," she said and squeezed each of their hands as she looked at them in turn.

"You have both been my greatest blessings. I will die peacefully now, knowing that you have each found your destiny. As for you, Bahr'Mok, do not be in a hurry to pair. Promise me you will take your time in choosing a mate," she said. "And most of all, make sure she loves you as you love her."

"Deparia," Hatos'Mok said and hung his head.

"Shhhhh. There is no need to talk of this. We have had a good life. I know you have loved me in your own way. And I have been honored to stand at your side. Now the mantle is passing to our sons. Let us pray they each live as rewarding a life as you and I have been fortunate to."

Word quickly circulated that Bahr'Mok would be taking over the Deep Valley. Preparations were made to clean up the assembly chamber and decorate it for the evening's ceremony. Many of the females were discussing the unexpected appointment of Bahr'Mok over his brother.

News of the pairing of Rohm'Mok and the Guardian were exchanged in small circles and quickly took on the making of a once-in-a-lifetime romance. Few knew the Guardian, so there was much room for speculation about their union. In contrast to Hatos'Mok's viewpoint of the situation, many felt there was a rightness about it all.

Bahr'Mok and his brother stood together in a small meeting room just outside the assembly area.

Bahr'Mok was readying himself for the ceremony about to take place. "Who would have thought it would be me and not you to whom Father will pass the 'Mok staff tonight," he said.

"I think I have always known. I have always seen greatness in you."

"I hope I do not disappoint you."

"You will not. Father will be at your side for many years yet to come. So while you take his counsel, remember also to be true to who you are. Not Father's idea of who you are. Or even Mother's. You must lead from your own soul, your own heart, your own wisdom."

"And what of you?"

"I will stay until Mother passes. Which I am afraid will not be too long. Then I will return to the High Rocks."

"Will it not be peculiar to be the mate of the Adik'Tar?" he asked.

"I will let you know."

They both smiled in a tiny moment of levity.

Bahr'Mok walked out ahead with his brother a few feet behind. So, the mantle of leadership now fell to him, not his brother as he had always believed it would. *Rohm has faith in me, just as Mother does.* Bahr'Mok would remember his brother's words of wisdom and try to set aside their father's last doubt in his abilities.

In the center of the assembly stood Hatos'Mok, the Leader's Staff in his hand. Deparia was seated not far from him, supported by the stone wall behind her.

"Today is the day that always eventually comes," began Hatos'Mok. "The day when leadership of a community passes from one hand to another.

"As every parent here knows, you cannot help but have dreams of what will become of your offling. You want the best for them, and sometimes your vision of what they should become does not match up with their desires. It is not a secret that since he was born, I imagined the House of 'Mok passing to my first son, Rohm'Mok. But the Great Spirit has another future for him. As you know, he has paired with the Guardian, Pan. And I wish him all the best in his new life at the High Rocks."

He motioned for Bahr'Mok to come forward and stand at his side.

"I have not handled Rohm'Mok's decision well. I have made it difficult for him and the rest of my family. And for that, I apologize. We have had words, ah, yes. If you are lucky, the time comes when your offling stand up to you and declare their right to choose their own paths. And then you know you have done your job as a parent. You have raised your offling to think for themselves, and though it may be difficult to give up your own idea of the path they should choose, you can find solace in knowing that they have come into their own and your job is complete."

"Bahr'Mok, you will be a great Leader of the people of Awenasa. You will guide them with wisdom and heart. Your patience and willingness to listen will prove to be only some of your many great gifts. Though you were not my first choice to assume leadership of the Deep Valley, I now realize you are the best choice. I am proud to hand the Leader's Staff to you."

He held the Leader's Staff out to Bahr'Mok, who reached across and firmly grasped it. Hatos'Mok then released the staff and declared, "*Kah-Sol 'Rin! It is done!*"

Bahr'Mok could see his mother supported by Krin, smiling at him with such love in her eyes. It brought the sting of tears, and he fought them back. *She will pass soon, I can feel it. This is what she was waiting for.*

He returned his attention to the crowd, looking out at many smiling faces and some serious ones. The Akassa stood toward the front with the larger Mothoc behind them. So much disparity. So little resemblance between the two groups. It was up to him now to find a way to bridge the future for all his people.

Bahr'Mok turned to his father and nodded before stepping out into the crowd and making his way to his mother. "You look tired. Do you need to retire for the evening?" he asked. She nodded, and with Krin, he carefully helped her stand.

"Stay here and mingle among your people, please," Deparia said. "Come and see me when you are done and wake me if I am sleeping. Promise me you will."

Bahr'Mok nodded and solemnly watched as Krin helped his mother make her way to the welcome rest that awaited her in her quarters. His father followed them soon after.

Well-wishers came up to have a word with the new Adik'Tar. Bahr'Mok gave them each their due of attention, and it was some time before the hall had cleared out. Rohm'Mok had stayed through it all, and Bahr'Mok was grateful for his brother's support.

Once almost everyone had left, Rohm'Mok approached him. "I do not know if you noticed, but you were being looked over very thoroughly by many of the younger females. I suspect you will have your pick now that you are Adik'Tar."

Bahr'Mok chuckled. "No doubt you are right. I will do my best to do as Mother said and take my time. I can only pray to be as blessed as you are to have found your beloved so young in your years."

"Trust me in this, brother," Rohm'Mok said. "No matter how long it takes, it is worth the wait."

Bahr'Mok nodded his agreement. "Let us go and see Mother now."

They found Krin waiting for them just outside the room. "What is wrong?" Bahr'Mok asked.

"I am glad you have come," she said. "She does not have long. We were about to send for you." She led them to their mother's sleeping mat.

Deparia slowly opened her eyes and watched as her sons entered. She weakly reached out her hand for them to come to her side.

Rohm'Mok and Bahr'Mok crouched down to her level. "Where is Father?" asked Rohm'Mok.

"He has been at my side until just now. We have

said our goodbyes. Now it is my time to be with you two," she said quietly.

"No, please. Do not leave us yet," said Bahr'Mok, taking her hand and raising it to press against his cheek.

"Shhhhh. We all know it is time for me to go. I do not wish to leave you, but I am at peace knowing you have each found your own paths, and I have no will to continue suffering; I long for release from this painful vessel."

"I love you so much," said Bahr'Mok.

Rohm'Mok held her other hand and could only nod in agreement.

"I know you do, both of you. You have been wonderful sons; no mother could ask for better. And no mother could ask for more than both of you have given me. I have loved you each from the moment I first held you in my arms. I heard you each take your first breath. I watched over both of you as you started to crawl, then as you took your first steps. I opened my arms to you after your first fall. Hearing your first words, learning your likes and dislikes, discovering along the way who you were. Oh! How you hated tarnosil sprouts, Bahr. I could hardly ever get you to eat them. And you, Rohm, how you wanted to do anything but follow your father around listening to his tales of the honors and triumphs of leadership."

They both smiled, acknowledging the truth of that.

She continued quietly, "I can leave happily,

knowing that when your father finally joins me, you will still have each other. You each have your own gifts. Even though you will be living in different places, never lose touch. Turn to each other, lean against each other. Every parent knows the time will come—after they have returned to the Great Spirit—when their offling will only have each other. And so we do our best to try to forge a bond between you, a bond that will carry you together into your future, long after we are no longer here. Remember this when you have your own offling. Do not raise them to compete or bicker among themselves. Teach them to honor their differences, to support each other in their individual gifts and life choices. To celebrate each other's victories and comfort each other in times of trial."

Exhausted, Deparia let out a huge sigh. She moaned and her body convulsed.

Both sons immediately glanced at Krin, who was watching solemnly from just inside the door. She nodded sympathetically.

They turned back to their mother. Finally, Deparia quieted and said, "Please do not cry too much for me. I will see you again; I know this to be true. Never forget how much I have loved you—and will always love you. Take care of each other."

She turned her head to the other side. "Please leave me now. I wish to be alone. But know that my love goes with you."

It was all Bahr'Mok could do to maintain some composure. "I love you, Mother."

"I love you as well. Good Journey." Rohm'Mok was also obviously battling to control the quiver in his voice.

Both rose, and Krin motioned for them to come to her.

"Let her have her last wish. Leaving this realm is a very private experience. Your mother is deeply spiritual, and she feels this in her soul."

She guided them through the doorway. "She will be gone by morning. Remember her words. Know that her love goes with you every step of the way, for the remainder of both of your lives. Honor her by honoring your own journey; it is all she has ever wanted. Take comfort in knowing that she lived to see her dreams come true, for each of you has found your path."

"Will you stay with her?" Rohm'Mok asked.

"I will make sure she knows I am right outside. As, shortly, my father will also be. If she calls out, I will go to her, I promise."

The two brothers thanked the young Healer and quietly walked down the corridor, each step taking them one bit farther away from the female who had spent her life preparing them for just this moment—when they would be left to walk into the future without her to guide and comfort them.

Early the next day, Oragur went to tell the sons that their mother had returned to the Great Spirit. The community was in mourning, and the two brothers spent the day outside together, away from everyone else, reminiscing about their upbringing and consoling each other.

Hatos'Mok spent his day in solitude. He prayed for his mate's forgiveness for his stubbornness. He thought back to their last hours together when he had again declared his love for her and expressed his regret that he had not been a better mate. Too late, he had learned what mattered, and he would spend the rest of his life regretting that he had not loved her more deeply. He was not the mate she deserved, but she had loved him, regardless.

Oragur and his mate, Neilith, made the ceremonial preparations. When it was time, everyone assembled, and Oragur conducted the ritual.

The ceremony over, Hatos'Mok nodded to his sons and went back to what had been his quarters with Deparia.

Alone.

CHAPTER 9

Back at Kthama, Pan tended to the business of running the High Rocks. The cold weather would eventually break, but in the meantime, hunting parties still went out to keep the stores full. The youngest offling played in the Great Chamber, watched over collectively by some of the mothers. Every morning, Pan checked her figure, looking to see if it was obvious yet that she was seeded. Luckily, her heavier winter coat covered much of her shape. When she was not busy, she spent much of her leisure time visiting Tyria and cuddling the Healer's offling.

"He is so good-natured. I hope I am as lucky—" Pan caught herself.

Tyria's eyes opened wide, "You are seeded?"

"Oh— Oh, I could not possibly know that already. I was just saying how calm your son is."

"Well, do not worry; it will happen in time."

Pan changed the subject. "How is Jhotin working out?"

"He is a big help to me. He is smart, learns fast, and is patient. He is also attentive and can see when I need a break. And he never complains about the time I take to tend to Fahr."

"He sounds like the perfect male."

Tyria eyed her friend and laughed. "Do not get any ideas, Guardian. I am not in any rush to be paired. I am just saying I appreciate his help."

The rebel group led by Laborn had managed to settle into a routine in their new location. The nearby stream did turn out to be a rich source of fish, and of course, fresh water. The vortex below was nowhere as strong as the one at Kthama and not likely to be the strongest they could have found, but the group had grown tired of travel and was satisfied with the new habitat.

Hunting was also plentiful. The nearby forest provided all they needed to build a life there for themselves. The females had made the living quarters as comfortable as could be, and several were seeded and awaiting the birth of their offling. As time went by, there was less grumbling about having to leave Kayerm, and it appeared that even their Leader was finally making peace with the past.

Laborn woke to screaming and jumped up from his mate's side. Billows of dust were blowing into their chamber. "Get up, get up! Something terrible is happening," he shouted.

He pulled his mate to her feet, and they both ran out into the tunnel, trying to wave the dust clouds away to see for sure where they were going.

Voices of males, females, and offling filled the interior, some yelling warnings and others calling for help. In the background was a rumbling and a terrible sound of falling, crashing rock.

Feeling his way along the side of the passage toward the very first rays of daylight coming in through the opening of the entrance, Laborn took Shikrin's hand and eventually led her out to safety. They were both coughing, and he wiped his face trying to clear the dust from his eyes. He spotted a gathering of his people a distance away and pointed to her to join them.

Kaisak and Gard came storming out of the entrance, turning back and yelling to others behind them who were also trying to escape.

Laborn ran over to them. "What happened? How many are left inside?"

"Several from what I can tell by the voices."

"Let the debris settle so we can see what we are doing," he ordered. "As soon as we can, we will go back in and get them out."

The wait was excruciating as they had to continue listening to the calls for help. Laborn went back to the entrance and stepped into it, calling out loudly, "Stay where you are. We will get you out as soon as we can!"

Hearing the voices, Shikrin cried out, "Hoontl is still in there, my dearest friend! Please go in and help her!"

"We will," Laborn shouted and ran back to her side. "But it is too dangerous to go in there now."

"No! We must help her! Now!" and Shikrin tore away from them all and ran toward the back caverns.

"No!" Laborn immediately followed after her. He choked and gasped as he entered the dust-filled entrance. Just then, there was another rumble, and the entrance started to collapse.

"Shikrin!" he called out, but rocks and more dust started raining down from the ceiling.

Laborn staggered clear of the entrance, and just as the ceiling at the back of the entrance collapsed, was dragged to safety by Kaisak. A giant dust cloud billowed out, and then the air was still, filled only with silence.

Laborn staggered to his feet and cried out, "Noooo!" then collapsed down to his knees, his head buried in his arms.

Several of the males ran to the opening and stood there, unable to help those trapped and now certainly crushed to death.

Useaves, the older female who served as their

Healer, came to console him and he shrugged her off as his grief quickly turned to anger.

Enraged, he staggered to his feet and raised his fist to the sky. "Moc'Tor! Straf'Tor! Why will you not let us be! We have all tried to move on; even I have. But now this. This is your fault. You brought this on us. You created the abominations that drove us from our home. I promise I will repay you for your crimes. I will not rest until all the PetaQ Akassa are scoured from the face of Etera!"

Having figured out who they had lost by who was not in the crowd outside the entrance, many others also started wailing.

"Laborn is right," Gard shouted to the others gathered outside. "If Straf'Tor and Moc'Tor had not angered the Great Spirit, none of this would have happened. We would all still be safe at Kthama, but because of *their* mistakes, we were driven from our home. First to Kayerm and then here. To this!"

"We must set it right! This must be our mission now. Despite this tragedy, despite our heartache, we must now all vow to live long enough to see them die!

Others in the crowd cried out in agreement.

"Let them continue on in their travesties!" Laborn bellowed. "The more the Akassa reproduce, the weaker they become. They are no match for us, even now, but we must focus on increasing our own numbers. Time is on our side. Mark my words; the day will dawn when we will have our revenge! When the time is right, they will surrender or die. *We will become their masters!*"

"But what of the Sassen!" Kaisak yelled out. "Are they also not an abomination? They are also proof of Staf'Tor and Moc'Tor's betrayal of the Others. The Others were our wards; it was our charge to protect them. Instead, our so-called Leaders betrayed their trust. As long as the Sassen live, it is a bloodstain on the honor of the Mothoc!"

"You are right!" shouted Laborn. "It is so clear now. We have become complacent. We have turned our focus away from the truth. And we have paid the price. But no longer. We must wake up and accept our calling! We must rid Etera of both the Akassa and the Sassen. Only then will we again find favor with the Great Spirit!"

Laborn dominated and overpowered his people. Nothing had ever been said about the dream they had all experienced; no one had dared mention it, fearing Laborn's anger. And so, lacking any other guidance, his words found fertile ground in the hearts of his followers. Their grief turned to hatred. Their devastation to anger. Their heartache turned to vengeance. They ignored and dismissed the Rah-hora.

The band of Mothoc rebels, born to the sacred service of Etera, had lost their way.

Unable to unearth their lost loved ones, Laborn performed the Good Journey before gathering his followers and heading west, following the magnetic lines in search of another home. Now driven by a bloodlust for revenge, he vowed the new location would be located over a vortex strong enough for them to become unbeatable in numbers and in strength. And though Laborn had lost his way, he had found his purpose, his reason to live. *Revenge.*

With his mother gone and his brother in place as Leader of the Deep Valley, Rohm'Mok took leave of his family and returned to his beloved at Kthama.

They spent the day of their reunion in Pan's quarters, trying to block out everything but their love for each other.

When they had finished their lovemating, Pan leaned back against Rohm'Mok's shoulder. "I said I would not speak of troubles, but there is something I cannot make peace with."

"What is it, my love?" Rohm'Mok asked, taking one of her hands and kissing her fingers.

"It is the Akassa. The future belongs to them, yet their Leader seems hesitant. Unsure of himself."

"It is also true at the Deep Valley. They do defer to us in all matters. I understand and share your concern. Perhaps it is time for us to step back. Perhaps we should try harder in some way to transfer authority to them in each of the communities."

"The time of tracing the genetic bloodline through the females has passed. It has returned to the males, and we must press the Akassa descendants of each house to take over their own communities. Here, that would be Takthan from Ny'on's line. Several of her daughters took up the call and were seeded by the Others, luckily, as that has preserved the 'Tor line in the Akassa."

Rohm'Mok gently put her hand down and then laid his own on her belly. "How is our offling coming along?"

"Whoever is in there, he or she is very calm, though it is still early days."

"While we have some time alone together, relax and let all your worries go," said her mate. "Today is ours. Tomorrow we can once more pick up our worries and troubles."

Pan did not want to burden Rohm'Mok with her concerns, but the offling's presence within her was so faint. She would have to talk with Tyria soon. *Great Spirit, please, let our offling be healthy.* Was it not enough that she had lost her father, her mother, and had to give up Liru to Oragur and his new mate? Why did it seem that she was being asked to give more of herself than she could almost bear?

A pang of guilt shot through Pan as she realized she had still not yet visited the Aezaiterian flow, nor the Order of Functions since her parents' deaths. *I hear your call, and in time I will surrender. But not yet. Not yet.*

Back at Kayerm, Nox'Tor had disappeared into the background of the community, splitting his time between his own tasks and slipping away to solitude in the little cave he had made his second home.

With Nox'Tor no longer in authority, Norland and Wosot fell into an easy stride together. A deep bond was forming between them, and they spent many hours discussing the future of the community. One of the greatest challenges was the rift between the males and females. It was clear that the females needed to pair and produce offling if the community was to survive. And it was not for their own sakes. That the Mothoc would vanish altogether at some point seemed inevitable, so for the sake of Etera, the Sassen must not.

"It seems the females are still reluctant to choose a male," said Norland. "We have so many who are ripe for seeding, yet they do not wish to pair. Do you have any insight?"

"I would say they fear subjugation. Despite their longing to have offling, I believe they perceive that a pairing would put them under the domination of a male," said Wosot.

"How do we fix that? And is it true? Are we so domineering that we would overshadow our mates' wishes without knowing it?" Norland picked up a twig and twirled it between his fingers.

"I believe their fears are warranted in some cases. It will take a while to undo the climate created by your father. He treated the females poorly. Forgive me, but it has to be said."

"I take no offense. You speak the truth. My father created an atmosphere of terror, passing females back and forth as if they were property. So it falls to all of us males. How do we gain their trust?"

Wosot thought a moment. "Consider my relationship with Lorgil. We are not paired, yet she benefits from my protection. And in turn, she helps provide for me by way of the female's contributions to any house. It is mutually beneficial with no imbalance of power between us. Perhaps if this model of the pod is offered to others, it will help our males gain the trust of the females."

"But without pairing, will the males agree to this? It is true that males have in the past had a pod of females, but it was not only as friends."

"It falls to us to make them understand it from the females' perspective, and that ultimately this is the only way to mend the damage that Nox'Tor created. Once the females see that they are being fairly treated, perhaps the rift will narrow."

"My grandmother's support would be beneficial," Norland said. "Shall we go speak with her about this?"

Wosot agreed, and they went in search of Toniss.

Toniss and Trak were just coming back from fishing in the shallows next to the riverbank. Norland let out a whoot call to get their attention.

The males stood and waited for Toniss and Trak to catch up to them. "May we have a word with you, Grandmother?"

"Two of my favorite males; what are you up to? Planning something, no doubt?" Then she held up her catch for them to admire.

"The spring waters are bringing us new blessings, I see," commented Wosot at the hearty longfish in Trak's basket.

"Come, walk with us, please," said Norland. "We need your advice."

Norland explained his and Wosot's theory about the females. When they were done, Toniss and Trak agreed that their idea would be a wise one to implement.

After another day of mulling it over, Norland called the males together to discuss what he was proposing. He helped them understand that with such an arrangement, perhaps in time, affection would grow between those in the pod, leading to pairing. Eventually, the majority of them agreed that such an arrangement with a female might be the only way to heal the division between them. Having gotten the males' consensus, Norland called an assembly to share the plan with the females.

Standing where his father, the great Straf-Tor, had stood many times to address the people of Kayerm, Norland explained his proposed alternative to pairing. When he was done speaking, Toniss stepped forward.

"Our Leader is wise; I urge you to consider his proposal. Aside from the physical pleasure and the desire for offling, males and females need each other in different ways. Wosot and Lorgil are proof that this arrangement can work. You can speak about it with them if you like."

Far in the back of the crowd, trying to be as inconspicuous as possible, Nox'Tor silently fumed. He stared at Lorgil as she and Wosot stepped to the forefront to make themselves available for questions. As she came into full view, Nox'Tor's brows lifted. He knew Lorgil's every curve, every bend in her physical landscape, and her swollen belly was as obvious to him as a black crow against a cloudy winter sky.

He clenched his fists and tried with all his might to control his anger. But when Wosot placed his hand on Lorgil's back to encourage her to step forward again, Nox'Tor's dammed-up anger broke.

"Lies. It is all lies!" he bellowed as he broke from the back and started to push his way forward.

"Your new leadership is lying to you! Do not be deceived by this false talk of the success of such an arrangement. My son presents Wosot and Lorgil as proof of the success of this so-called platonic pod. Yet, in truth, Wosot has placed his seed in Lorgil! Admit it!"

The crowd parted for him, and within moments he was at the front, marching up to Wosot.

"Traitor! Liar. I know that female. I lay with her many times; I know every inch of her. You have seeded her. What you are is a farce!"

Nox'Tor then turned to Lorgil to confront her. "Admit it! Admit it! You are with offling!"

"I do not deny it!" Lorgil shouted back, laying protective hands on her belly.

"See!" Nox'Tor shouted. "She admits to it. They wish to sell you a concept they themselves, the shining example of this arrangement, could not honor. Lorgil is seeded!"

"I have not touched her!" Wosot stated firmly in return. "You dishonor her and me with your false accusations. I had hoped you might change, Nox'Tor. But I can see now that it will never happen."

"You are the one who stands here covered in dishonor. Even now, with the proof in her expanding belly, you still deny the truth?" Nox'Tor moved toward Lorgil.

Before he could take another step, Wosot sprang forward and jerked him back.

Lorgil turned to the others present. "Wosot speaks the truth. There has been nothing between us except mutual assistance. He has never once touched me. The offling is not his; it is Nox'Tor's."

She took a step toward her prior mate, knowing that Wosot had him firmly in hand. "The offling is *yours*," she repeated. "I was seeded when you discarded me. You threw me away for being barren, not knowing that even as you rejected me, I was carrying your offling."

"No! You would have told me!" he shouted.

"I would have told you, had you given me the chance. Instead, you were too busy forcing your will on us—that every female had to choose a mate whether she wanted to or not—and treating us like property. When you cast me aside, whatever I might have owed you as the father of my offling, your heartless actions forfeited."

Nox'Tor snarled and spat at Lorgil from within Wosot's strong grip.

Toniss stepped between Lorgil and Nox'Tor, forcing Lorgil to step back.

"Enough of this," she shouted. "Enough! Lorgil speaks the truth. We all saw it. You blamed her for being barren and cast her aside, intending to take a third mate. You forced her on Wosot, intending to punish them both, yet luckily for her, Wosot is an honorable male who has taken Lorgil in and done nothing but provide for her and treat her with respect. Something you never did for her or, lately, Kyana, either."

Nox'Tor struggled to break free. "I will never believe it. Not until I see the offling freed from her water cradle!"

Norland spoke up. "Have it your way, then. Refuse to accept the truth, but in your refusal, stay clear of Lorgil. You are not to go near her. If you do, I will banish you from Kayerm."

"You would banish your own father?" Nox'Tor frowned and glared at his son.

"If you leave me no choice. Yes. This is not about our relationship. This is about what is best for Kayerm. For all of us. I urge you to return to the life you have created by your own hand and do not make matters worse for yourself."

"Let me go," said Nox'Tor, twisting to look up at Wosot. Norland nodded, and Wosot released his hold. Nox'Tor staggered a bit with the change in momentum.

He briefly opened his mouth as if to say something to Wosot, then took one last look around, his eyes lidded with anger, and stormed off.

The tension in the crowd lifted, and some chatter started up. Norland let it continue for a while before calling them back to order.

"Listen to me. Consider my proposal. Take some time, both males and females, to find your own understanding of the wisdom in this arrangement. Whether we return to any male having more than one female remains to be seen. But if it comes to that, it will still always be at the females' discretion. Now, go in peace. We will talk again."

The crowd slowly dispersed, many looking back at Wosot and Lorgil, discussing among themselves this last turn of events. Whatever sympathies arose for Nox'Tor, he seemed by his own actions to extinguish them each time.

Several of the females encircled Lorgil, congratulating her on being seeded. To the side, knowing he could not see her, Kyana studied Wosot.

He was a good male. It did not matter that he was older; any female would be blessed to stand at his side. What was she to do? When Lorgil delivered, what male would step up to protect and help raise the infant? The obvious answer was Wosot. He was kind and protective, and Lorgil was already under his care.

Kyana was filled with concern. She knew that shared kindnesses brought people close, and it was clear that Wosot and Lorgil were helping each other on a daily basis. If she waited too long to decide, though there was no heat between Wosot and Lorgil at present, it was possible the relationship between them might catch fire.

Toniss and Trak remained behind to speak with Norland.

Once they were alone, Norland looked at his grandmother. "This is the hardest thing I have ever done. He is still my father. If there were problems between my mother and him, I was not aware of them. And then, when Straf'Tor left, it changed him.

He became harsh and cruel. He turned into someone I have never known."

Toniss smiled kindly at the young male who had been forced to grow up so quickly. "You come from greatness. And you have greatness within you."

Norland frowned.

"The blood of 'Tor runs in your veins," Toniss clarified, seeing the confusion on his face. "Look past your father's failings and remember who you are."

"How are Dotrat, Lai, and Somnil coping?" Trak asked.

"Dotrat is angry. He is confused by everything that has happened. Right now, he hates our father for how he treated Mother—and for hurting Lorgil. I pray it does not make him bitter. Being females, Lai and Somnil are naturally close to Mother, so the shock is not as great. But they are also affected, to be sure."

"She loves him," Toniss said. "Your mother loves Wosot."

"I know," Norland admitted. "And he loves her."

"But she loves all of you more," added Trak. "Her first duty will always be to her offling."

Norland tilted his head, then looked down. When he looked back up at them, he had understood what Trak was trying to tell him.

Norland found his siblings enjoying a break from their daily tasks. Dotrat was stretched out in the newly sprouting tall grasses, enjoying the fresh breeze drifting across from the river. Lai and Somnil were competing to see who could stack some river stones the highest before they toppled over. As Norland approached, he took a moment to enjoy the sound of his sisters' laughter against the noise of the passing waters.

Dotrat sat up at seeing Norland. "Greetings, brother!"

Norland waved and continued his approach.

"Should you not be out doing something Leaderly?" Dotrat good-naturedly chided his brother.

Norland chuckled, "Probably. But I thought I should do something more important, such as check in on you all." He sat down. "It is so pleasant here, far from the worries of the day."

"I am sorry you have worries," said Dotrat. "I am not blind to the situation. He is, after all, still our father—as Mother keeps reminding us."

Norland sighed. "What do you think of all that is going on? Please, speak your heart."

"My allegiance is not as torn as yours—though, perhaps allegiance is not the proper word. I do not know when I will be able to forgive him."

"She loves Wosot, you know. And he loves her." Norland looked over at his brother.

"You are saying that they belong together? But she hesitates because of—us?"

"That is my belief."

"Then we must reassure her. She deserves happiness. Everyone does."

"You are wise. Are you sure you are not the elder brother?"

"You forget; I was not without influence. Recently, as I have been thinking about our upbringing, I realized that in many ways, Wosot was more involved with us than Nox'Tor ever was."

Dotrat's use of their father's name threw the truth of the situation up in Norland's face. Was Dotrat right? Wosot did seem to have been involved with them all a great deal. *I wonder if he has loved Mother all along, and we, being young, just did not see it.*

Wosot, Lorgil, and Kyana were enjoying a late afternoon walk along one of the higher elevations surrounding Kayerm. They chatted as they looked along the way for food stuffs to fill the carrying baskets. Wosot was holding his fishing spear and had added some longfish to their spoils. Lorgil walked with one hand rested on her expanding belly, and Wosot knew that she was delighting in the feel of the life within her.

As they turned a corner, they looked up to see the dark figure of Nox'Tor blocking their path.

Concerned, Wosot immediately stepped in front of Kyana and Lorgil.

"I only wish to pass," Nox'Tor said.

"Then pass," Wosot said, not wanting trouble with Lorgil and Kyana there. He stepped to the side, though he put a protective arm out across the females.

Nox'Tor walked by, then stopped and turned back.

"You think you have won. You have both my females, it is true. But only for the moment, I assure you."

"Drop this, Nox'Tor," Wosot warned. "It will only lead to your banishment. What has been done was by your own hand. It was you who cast both Lorgil and Kyana aside."

"Perhaps, but you lost no time claiming them both," Nox'Tor snarled.

"It was you who forced Lorgil into my care. As for Kyana, she has the right to choose with whom she wishes to associate. I have touched neither, I assure you."

"Lorgil's belly says otherwise."

Lorgil stepped out from behind Wosot, away from his protection. "It is your offling, Nox'Tor, who grows inside me. Wosot speaks the truth."

"For all of our sakes," said Wosot, "I urge you to move on. Build a new life for yourself."

"*Bacht!*" Nox'Tor stepped back toward them and spit on the ground in front of Wosot. "And how is that possible? None of the females will have me; you have made sure of that by your slander."

Kyana also stepped out in front of Wosot. "I cannot remain silent; all that has happened has been your own doing. Please, let us be. We are none of your concern any longer."

Nox'Tor glared at Kyana, then let his gaze run over her, up and down. "Come back to me." He locked his eyes on her. "Come back to me and let it be as it once was between us."

"It can never be as it once was," Kyana said softly. "The person who loved you no longer exists. She died at your own hand, by your treatment of her."

"So now you love Wosot? Is that it? You are content to take second place in his bed? Watching Lorgil raise his offling while you have no more of your own?" he taunted her.

"I will not listen to your lies any longer." Kyana turned to Wosot, her eyes filled with fear.

"What do you look to him for? I am your mate; he is not, and if I cannot have you, then no one will." Nox'Tor lunged at Lorgil, who was closest to him, and shoved her to the ground.

As Wosot turned to help Lorgil, Nox'Tor grabbed Kyana, threw her over his shoulder, and ran toward the cliff.

"No!" Wosot seized the fishing spear and ran after Nox'Tor, with Lorgil following as quickly as she could.

Kyana began clawing at Nox'Tor's head and face. "Put me down, stop it, stop it!" she screamed as she scraped and bit at whatever part of him was within reach.

Nox'Tor called out in pain and raised his hands to protect his face. Off-balance, they both tumbled to the ground, and on all fours, Kyana scrambled away as quickly as she could.

Having closed the distance between them, Wosot tossed his spear aside and threw himself at Nox'Tor. The two males rolled on the ground, snarling and growling as each sought advantage over the other.

As they struggled and rolled, Nox'Tor spied the discarded fishing spear just beyond reach and instead fought his way out of Wosot's hold long enough to grab it and jump to his feet. Before Wosot could react, Nox'Tor had him pinned to the ground with the deadly tip pressed against his throat. Wosot stared up at his enemy, weighing his next move.

"Stop it! Stop it!" Kyana cried out. "Stop it, and I will go with you. Willingly. Hear me, Nox'Tor!"

"You will return to my bed, never to leave again?" Nox'Tor shouted, pressing the tip harder, never taking his eyes off Wosot. "You will yield to me as my mate? Say it. Say it!" A small trickle of Wosot's blood leaked onto the ground.

"Yes! Yes!" she pleaded. "I will yield to you as your mate!"

Nox'Tor fleetingly glanced at Kyana. "You lie. You say this only to spare his life. It is he you love."

And he prepared to drive the spear through Wosot's neck.

"Nox'Tor!" Lorgil called out.

He paused. She was standing at the cliff's edge.

"Release him. Release him, or I take your offling over the ledge with me."

"You are mad. Go ahead and die, then. It is not my offling. I am not a fool to be tricked by another lying female!"

"It is your offling. Look at my belly. Think. It is obvious by how far along I am that it is your son whom I carry!"

Nox'Tor stared down at Wosot, who was watching intently, looking for an opportunity to make a move.

"You said it yourself!" Lorgil continued shouting. "No other female will have you. You have lost the respect of your offling by Kyana. If I die, your only chance at having a son who does not hate you dies with me."

"Come here," Nox'Tor ordered. "Walk over to me, now!"

"Remove the spear from Wosot's throat first."

Nox'Tor did not comply but instead glanced over at Kyana. "You. Come here."

Kyana stepped over to his side, and in a single movement, Nox'Tor pulled her in front of him, dragged her backward a few steps, and repositioned the spear across her body, so she was trapped against him. He then quickly tossed the spear aside, whipped out a hunting knife from a sash around his waist, and pressed it against Kyana's throat.

Wosot had risen to his feet, never looking away from Nox'Tor.

"Move back. Do not test me unless you wish to see this female's blood spilled in front of your eyes," Nox'Tor snarled.

Then he addressed Lorgil. "It is now or never. Either jump to your death or come here to me."

Lorgil stepped away from the ledge and walked toward Nox'Tor.

"Stand next to me, but be warned, if you try anything, my knife will open Kyana's throat," Nox'Tor shouted.

When Lorgil finally stood beside him, he laughed, "I now have both your females, Wosot! It is I who have won."

Wosot and Kyana exchanged quick glances.

Nox'Tor's face twisted even more. "But I am not the fool you think I am; neither of these will ever be true to me. I can see my victory is an illusion, so you leave me no choice. I will not rest until I have disposed of both these females, forever. Say goodbye to Kyana, Wosot."

Kyana had slowly positioned her right hand while Nox'Tor was distracted, and just as he made to draw the knife across her throat, she grabbed him between his legs and twisted as hard as she could.

Nox'Tor screamed and dropped the knife, clutching his seed pack and howling in pain. Kyana ran from his side toward Wosot, who was at the same time running to them. Though doubled over,

Nox'Tor managed to grab Lorgil's foot before she could flee.

He twisted her ankle until she fell to the ground next to him. Though still in pain, he crawled close enough to begin punching her, hard, in the stomach.

"No!" Kyana screamed.

Wosot leaped for the spear and dragged Nox'Tor away from Lorgil, but he tore himself away, screaming that he would kill her. Knowing he had no choice, Wosot raised the spear and drove it through Nox'Tor's heart, leaving him writhing in violent death throes.

Kyana ran to Lorgil, who was now curled into a tight ball, clutching her belly.

"No, no, no!" cried Kyana. "Oh, please, Great Spirit, no!" She took off in the direction of Kayerm. "We need Pagara!" she shouted back to Wosot.

Wanting to go to Lorgil's side but needing to ensure that Nox'Tor was dead, Wosot stood over the male who had once been his Leader. A giant red pool of blood seeped out from under Nox'Tor's body, which was deathly still. Wosot nudged the body with his foot, and seeing no response, knelt down to check for any signs of remaining life.

He startled when Nox'Tor opened his eyes.

"I am sorry it has come to this," Wosot said. "There was a time when our people believed you to be our next hope. That you would walk in the steps of your father and lead us into a future of our own making. Instead, you have turned away everyone who loved you. Because you could not see your own part in our future, your end was just a matter of time. The only saving grace was that it did not fall to Norland to put a stop to your reign of terror. No son should ever have to kill his own father. Good Journey, son of Straf'Tor. I pray you find peace in the next life."

And with that, Wosot watched as the light faded from Nox'Tor's eyes. Nox'Tor, son of Straf'Tor, was gone.

Assured that Nox'Tor presented no further threat, Wosot turned to Lorgil, who had stopped squirming in pain but still lay curled in a ball. He smoothed her forehead. "Stay with me. Help is coming," he softly said to her.

Before long, he heard the sound of running footsteps, and relief filled his heart as he saw Pagara, Toniss, and Trak running toward him, gamely followed by Kyana.

Pagara was immediately at Lorgil's side. The males turned away, giving Pagara privacy to examine Lorgil.

Pagara tried to get Lorgil to uncurl herself and roll over on her back but to no avail. The Healer gently examined her as best she could. "We need to get her home. We have no choice but to move her. Please."

She looked at the males.

Wosot, being the largest and strongest, knelt down and gently cradled Lorgil in his arms. They all walked back together, Wosot doing his best not to jostle her while getting back to Kayerm as quickly as possible.

Wosot shouted orders and directions as he carried Lorgil into Kayerm. Several males left with Trak to retrieve Nox'Tor's body, and despite his treasonous acts, would prepare it for the ritual of the Good Journey.

The Healer insisted on checking Kyana as well to make sure she had not been hurt. While both were in the Healer's Quarters under Pagara's care, Wosot went to find Norland.

Having been told by Wosot what had happened, Norland immediately whisked his siblings to a secluded area. He wanted to tell them their father was dead before they heard about it elsewhere.

"Sit by me," he told Dotrat, Lai, and Somnil. Somnil, the littlest one, crawled into his lap, and he cuddled her to him.

"We are about to go through a very difficult time," he started. "There is no gentle way to tell you, but our father is dead." He looked at them for their reaction before continuing.

"There was a fight between him and Wosot.

Father threatened both Mother and Lorgil, and though Wosot tried to avoid it, in order to protect them, he had to kill Father. I am very sorry to have to tell you this," he said, then looked down at Somnil, snuggled in his lap looking up at him.

Alarmed, Lai asked, "Where is Mother? Why is she not here with us?"

"Mother is alright. She is back at Kayerm. The Healer is just making sure she was not harmed."

"And Wosot?"

"Wosot is fine. But in the fight, our father did harm to Lorgil. The Healer is with her; we must pray she does not lose her offling."

Dotrat frowned angrily. "I am glad he is dead. He was mean to Mother; he did not love her or us!" He picked up a stone at his feet and threw it as hard as he could, and the sound of it hitting one of the nearby boulders pierced the silence.

"I know you are hurt and angry," said Norland, reaching out and placing a hand on his brother's shoulder.

"No, I mean it. I am glad he is dead. I hope I never hear anyone speak of him again," Dotrat repeated, shrugging off his brother's hand.

"Have your anger, Dotrat. You are entitled to it, but let it pass when it is time. Do not nurse it and let it take root in your soul. Emotions are like the weather; if allowed to, they will change because they are also energy. Right now, you are hurt and angry, and rightfully so. But in time, your feelings will shift.

Allow this transformation. Do not hold on to them and thus embitter yourself, lest you fall to our father's fate. It was Father's anger at his own father that took him down the path to his demise."

Norland looked at Dotrat and prayed that these words would find fertile soil in his soul.

⁂

Back at Kayerm, in quarters that Lorgil now shared with Kyana, Pagara did her best to make Lorgil comfortable, giving her what she could to ease the pain without harming the offling. The Healer, Kyana, and Toniss stayed by Lorgil's side while she slept.

Finally, Lorgil slowly opened her eyes. She reached out, and Kyana moved closer.

"My offling. Please tell me it is okay," she begged. Kyana looked back at Pagara.

"I am not able to tell you that; I am so sorry. Only time will tell if there was damage inflicted. It could go either way at this point," Pagara said quietly, resting her hand on Lorgil's forehead.

"Even if the offling survives," she started, "I do not wish to add to your heartache, but perhaps you should consider letting it go to return to the Great Spirit."

Lorgil frowned. "Let it go? What do you mean?"

"There are herbs. Medicines that can let your offling be released from your inner cradle. Its soul will then return to rest in the arms of the Great

Mother. If you do not lose it, you must consider this option, Lorgil. You may otherwise be dooming it to life as a cripple, or worse."

Tears started streaming down the sides of Lorgil's face, and she whimpered. Kyana took her hand and held it tightly.

"I will not kill my offling. If the Great Spirit spares its life, I will love it, raise it and protect it, no matter what," she said.

Kyana looked at Pagara as, for the first time in her life, she began to understand the burden of the Healer's mantle.

Her heart heavy, Toniss left the group to update those waiting outside for news. Her son was gone. Deep inside, she wondered where she had failed him and if she could have done more to help him. Perhaps the day would come when she would find peace about how his life turned out, but today was not that day. The possibility of losing his latest unborn offling only added to her heartache. Knowing there answers she sought were beyond her reach, she turned to that which had consoled her through all the prior challenges she had already endured—her faith. "Whatever happens is in the hands of the Great Spirit," she said.

By the next day, the Good Journey ritual had been held for Nox'Tor. It was a solemn occasion as many remembered the great promise shown by him, the son of Straf'Tor and Toniss. And they grieved not only the tragedy that his life had become but also the loss of the Leader he could have been.

Norland had stood looking at the body of the father he had once looked to for guidance in his own journey to becoming a male of honor. He prayed for himself, that the Great Spirit would correct him in his ways. *Above all, teach me to hear your voice. Help me to guide these people into the future of their making so that your divine plan may be fulfilled for the good of all those who follow you.*

Despite the damage Nox'Tor had inflicted during his limited reign as Leader, many of the community grieved his death, whereas others felt only relief that the climate of trouble and strife would hopefully now end, forever.

Back in Kyana's quarters, Lorgil had begun resting more comfortably, propped with additional hides and bedding into as comfortable a position as possible.

Pagara gave her something to drink. "You are not past risk, nor is your offling, though I am relieved you are able to rest without herbs to ease your pain. However, you have a long way to go. If Nox'Tor had not forbidden the use of the A'Pozz plant and made sure all my stores were destroyed, you would have suffered much less. My best advice is that you remain here with as little movement as possible until you deliver your offling."

"It is a son," Kyana offered. "She told Nox'Tor during the battle."

Lorgil shook her head. "I told him that because it is what I believe to be true. But I do not know it."

Kyana nodded, understanding that to give the offling a gender was a way to make it more real to Nox'Tor.

She turned her head to hide the stinging tears. *Oh, Nox'Tor. I did love you at one time. I am so sorry; I am so sorry. I pray you have found peace now in the House of the Great Spirit."*

The community had been assembled. Nearly everyone was in attendance except Pagara and Lorgil. The communal hearing regarding Wosot's killing of Nox'Tor was about to begin.

Norland, as Leader, Teirac, and three community members chosen at random would sit in judgment of Wosot's actions. The rest of the community was allowed to attend and even allowed to speak up at the proper time, either in support of or against Wosot's actions. Wosot had broken one of their laws, and that could not go without consideration, no matter what the consensus was regarding his actions.

Norland opened the meeting, "We are here

because one of our own has committed an act which may be in violation of Sacred Law. Our law states that no hand may be raised against another except for protection or defense. In a moment, Wosot will tell you from his viewpoint what happened. Then others will speak. The question, in this case, is whether Wosot had the right to kill Nox'Tor in defense not of himself but of the two females, Kyana and Lorgil, and Lorgil's unborn offling.

Norland then called Wosot to tell the story of what had taken place. When he was finished, Kyana was called up. Lorgil had sent her statement with Beala, who had been Ushca's best friend and was revered as one of the Elders.

The story of what had happened had already spread through the community. Norland had no question in his heart or mind that Wosot's actions were justified. Nor did he believe anyone thought or felt differently. But because Nox'Tor was Norland's father and Wosot was now Norland's right-hand male, it was even more important to follow a formal process to officially excuse Wosot's actions. Norland was a just and fair Leader, and he wanted no appearance of prejudice to cause his people to lose faith in his leadership.

After the details had been shared, the hearing was opened up for questions and statements. One of the younger males came forward to ask Wosot a question.

"At the time that you took Nox'Tor's life, did you want to kill him?"

Wosot looked over at Kyana, his beloved. "Yes. Yes, I wanted to kill him."

The crowd gasped at Wosot's admission as one person turned to another. Kyana caught her reaction in time and said nothing.

"So you admit you wanted to kill him. Everyone knows you favor Kyana—and have for a long time. Were you just waiting for the opportunity to get him out of the way so you could have her?"

"Nox'Tor had already rejected Kyana. Many of you heard it. He set aside his pairing to her, just as he did with Lorgil. I did not need to kill Nox'Tor to be with Kyana," Wosot answered.

"But it made it easier, did it not? To have him permanently out of the way?"

"Yager, how many have you killed?" Wosot asked.

"None. You know that."

"Then until you have, do not speak of how easy it is to take another's life. Despite our differences, killing Nox'Tor was the last thing I would have chosen to do."

There were no more questions, but Toniss asked to speak.

"I was—am—Nox'Tor's mother. Nox'Tor was a good-natured child; he got along with others, he learned easily. In all respects, he seemed to be the same as any of us, except that he had little confidence. I did not realize then what effect that would have on him as he grew up. You all know when his father died, Nox'Tor changed drastically. I believe it was because he did not know how to lead and so mimicked Straf'Tor's heavy hand without the experience and wisdom to temper it. Simply put, he made a mess, and he knew no other way to fix it than to continue to dominate and dictate without consideration for others."

Toniss looked out across the crowd. Everyone was listening intently.

"You all know me. I am not the most demonstrative female. I am sure some even say behind my back that I am cold. I have moments where I can express tenderness, but it is not my natural reaction. Perhaps, had I been a more openly loving mother, Nox'Tor would not have handled his problems so cold-heartedly. No mother wants to lose her son—or any of her offling. But as I look back at my son's path, I have to say that it seemed this would, at some point, be the likely outcome, whether by Wosot's hand or another's."

The mothers in the crowd felt an affinity with Toniss, fully understanding the self-blame that comes when one's offling has difficulties in life.

Breaking the silence, Beala asked to speak.

"We have all been through so much. Ushca's death, Straf'Tor's disappearance, and even before that, our exodus from Kthama and the other communities. Leaving homes we grew up in and were all we knew, leaving family and friends—and all over a divergence in philosophies. The laws are there to guide us, and on the surface, the law does not seem to excuse Wosot's actions because he was not defending himself. But there is also the sixth law: *Protect Those In Need.* I do not think any of us doubt that Nox'Tor was capable of killing Kyana and Lorgil. The fact that he hit Lorgil, trying to harm her and her offling, is proof of that."

She turned to Yager. "You are young and untested. And it was not an unfair question to ask if Wosot wanted to kill Nox'Tor. In the heat of the moment, seeing a huge male attacking a female, with or without offling—I am sure many here would have the same reaction. But do not confuse the desire to stop a wrong with the justification for doing so."

There was silence as Beala's words hung in the air.

After everyone had a chance to speak, Norland, Teirac, and the three others walked off to discuss their decision in private.

Kyana went over to Wosot and placed her hand on his heart. "You did what you had to do to protect us, and I will always be grateful to you for that."

Wosot placed his hand over hers and looked into her eyes; there were so many things he wanted to say to her. But then, those making up the tribunal came back.

One of the three community members spoke. "We have come to a decision. Having heard from the witnesses the story of what happened as well as the discussions among those present, we have decided that Wosot acted properly and there will be no punishment for the killing of Nox'Tor."

A sense of relief seemed to pass through everyone there. Though not necessary, Norland added, "This decision is binding on all. Anyone found acting aggressively or punitively against Wosot for Nox'Tor's death will be judged for his or her actions. Wosot, you are free to continue your life's path."

Kyana let out a long breath, until then not even realizing she had been holding it.

CHAPTER 10

Pan stood before the Mothoc High Council, Rohm'Mok at her side.

"Greetings. Today I speak to you of a matter of great importance. Perhaps the matter of most importance since my parents left us. When Kthama Minor was closed, we all received the same message."

The crowd murmured at her mention of Kthama Minor.

"Hear me now. The future belongs to the Sassen and the Akassa. We know it. We know it has to be this way. But that does not mean the Mothoc will perish from Etera. We must continue to serve the Great Spirit, yet our leadership of the Akassa is an impediment to that end."

Those facing her, the Mothoc Leaders from the other communities, murmured among themselves.

Pan raised the Leader's Staff and brought it down

onto the chamber floor with a resounding crack, and heads snapped back to face the front.

"Look around at your own communities, and you will realize the wisdom of my words. Our people are split. Through the ages, the division has become complete, and there exist now the Mothoc and the Akassa. But we are not equals, no. Not only do the Akassa defer to our leadership, our judgment, but they act as if they are subservient to us. Their Leaders do not even attend these meetings any longer. The Akassa step out of our way as we walk down the hallways. They take their meals at other times or at opposite sides of the chamber. They sweep their offling from our path. You all know this to be true. In all manner of behavior, they are showing us that they do not see themselves as our equals. And if they are not our equals, then they will always defer to us and will never lead themselves."

The others nodded, agreeing that what she said was true.

"What is your suggestion?" asked Hatos'Mok. The harsh edge to his voice was gone, mellowed by the passing of his mate.

"The Akassa need our help," said Pan. "We must step back; we must force them to assume leadership over themselves—demand that they do. The Akassa received the Rah-hora. They know what is laid before them, to make amends with the Others and to call them their Brothers. To learn their language and gain their trust. You know who these Leaders are in each of your communities, and you know they are not participating in leading. Think about what I have said, and we will continue this discussion at the next High Council Meeting."

"Thank you, Guardian." Tres'Sar of the Far High Hills spoke up. "Your wisdom is great. You have spoken that which I believe we all know in our hearts to be true. We have seen it demonstrated in our own communities. I, for one, acknowledge your inspired guidance in this matter."

"I want to raise a point, but not as a challenge, Guardian," said Tyria.

"Speak, Healer," Pan answered.

"The Akassa do not have our abilities. They do not seem to be as aware of the magnetic current that webs throughout Etera. Neither do they have as robust a seventh sense as we do. A few, mostly females, have more abilities here and there than others, but it is nowhere near as developed as ours, and it seems to have little correlation to their bloodlines. So, how will their Healers be chosen? And who will choose?"

"If I understand you, you are saying that a Healer's abilities are not being carried through a particular bloodline?"

Tyria nodded, "Yes, that is the quandary. If we cannot depend on the bloodlines to produce the Healers, then how will they manifest?"

Rohm'Mok spoke up. "You have said their seventh sense is not as developed as ours, but that does not mean it is nonexistent, just that it is weak by comparison. Yet that is all they have known; to them, there is not a deficiency. Think about Tensil. You told me yourself, she came to you because she felt called to it, despite not having as strong a seventh sense as any Mothoc. It is possible that the Akassa Healers will have to rely more on feeling a calling and on the understanding of natural remedies. If so, then instruction above intuition will be their mainstay.

"Just as we know the abilities of those within our community, so will the Akassa learn the gifts and strengths of their own. It will fall to them to watch for signs of an emerging Healer and select that person regardless of bloodline. They may not have as strong a seventh sense as we do, but it is not entirely lacking."

Pan nodded her agreement and waited for replies, scanning the faces before her.

Once the meeting was dismissed, Rohm'Mok and Pan took sanctuary in their private quarters.

"What you told them was not all of your plan, was it?" Rohm'Mok chuckled.

"You know me so well already?" She smiled and stepped into his embrace.

"So what else are you thinking?" he asked, kissing the top of her head.

"There is so much to be done. But the changes

must take place in their own time. There is more than I told the High Council; you are right. The Akassa, we intimidate them. We are separate from them, and unfortunately, in their estimation, are superior in most ways. My fear is that they will never lead themselves as long as we walk among them."

A chill passed through Rohm'Mok as the meaning of his mate's words reverberated through his soul. They were to leave the Akassa? It would not be enough for only a few Mothoc to leave. It must be all or none. But when? And where would they go?

Pan interrupted his thoughts. "Your relationship with your father? Is it repaired?"

"I believe so."

"My father trusted him, and I feel we must too. I need his support for what is to come," Pan said.

Pan, her mate, and Hatos'Mok stood sequestered in a private room.

"I will be blunt. Father trusted you, and I need to know now if I can do the same?" said Pan.

Hatos'Mok glanced at his son, hoping for some hint of what this was about. Finding none, he turned back to the Guardian.

"You have my support. Whatever issues there were between us were due to my ignorance. I promise that you can count on me from now on."

"Who is your most skilled watcher?"

"Skilled in what way?"

"Skilled in attunement to the vortex. To the magnetic currents that web through Etera."

Hatos'Mok looked at his son, "Asolp."

Rohm'Mok nodded and turned to Pan. "I agree."

"Is there a second?" Pan asked.

"Yes. B'Hit," Hatos'Mok answered.

"Can they be trusted? The future of Etera may rest on the success of what I am about to ask of them."

Hatos'Mok spoke. "Yes, Guardian; they can both be trusted."

"When you return to the Deep Valley, send them out into Etera," instructed Pan. "Have them follow the magnetic lines. I need them to find the strongest vortex aside from the one here at Kthama. Once they find it, have them locate a livable cave system and resources necessary to establish a community as close to the vortex as possible. Then they are to return to you with the location. It does not matter how far away it is. It does not matter how long their journey. Wherever this mission takes them, and for however long it may be before they return, it will be as it must. Do you have any questions?"

"No," Hatos'Mok replied. Then he added, "Guardian, no matter our past differences and your current doubts, you are the Leader High Rocks needs."

"Thank you. Now, please, return to your home. I

will await the news you will bring me at the appointed time."

<hr>

After his father had left, Rohm'Mok turned to his mate, "You look tired. Though still beautiful," he added quickly.

Pan chuckled. "Apparently, being the Guardian and trying to solve all of Etera's problems while creating a new life within me is more taxing than I anticipated."

Rohm'Mok laughed and pulled her into his embrace. "I believe you are divinely led by the Great Spirit. If anyone can lead us through this, it is you. *Way-shower*," he affectionately teased her about the meaning of her name.

Pan hugged her mate tightly as a shot of guilt ran through her soul. Could she? Would she really? She had turned her back on that which her father had relied on the most—the Aezaiterian flow and the Order of Functions. Perhaps, after all, it was time to set aside her resistance to her destiny.

<hr>

Over the upcoming few months, Pan and Rohm'Mok continued their private discussions about the future of the Akassa. They laid out a detailed approach, which, at the next High Council meeting, they would share with the Mothoc Leaders and Healers as a strategic plan for shifting leadership to the Akassa.

Pan's offling continued to develop within her. Tyria assured Pan that she still believed all was well, even though there was little movement from the tiny being.

"There has never been a female Guardian," the Healer explained. "But I see little reason to believe your experience should progress any differently than any other female. Please try not to worry—though I know it is difficult and easier said than done."

"What concerns me are the duties as Guardian that I have neglected. After my parents' death, I have hardened my heart against the Great Spirit. I am ashamed to tell you this."

Tyria remained silent, waiting for her friend to continue.

"I have not engaged with the Aezaiteria since my father's death. Nor have I engaged the Order of Functions, but now that I am seeded, I fear the effect it may have on my offling."

"If it is of the Great Spirit, how can it be detrimental to your offling? It seems it would only be beneficial."

"The Aezaiterian flow, perhaps. But the Order of Functions—it is an experience I struggle to explain. It is as if you are being taken apart, bit by bit—even to your consciousness—and stretched across eternity. Then, just as you cannot bear it a moment longer, you are brought back to yourself. At first, when I entered the Order of Functions with my father, it was only for brief visits because of how excruciating it was. As time went on, I was able to bear longer and longer stretches."

"It hurts?" Tyria asked.

"Not in a physical sense. In a soul sense. Like being on the precipice of non-existence. At first, it is quite frightening. Over time, as I knew what to expect, my fear decreased. But in no way would I ever describe it as pleasurable. At its best, it is only barely tolerable. After joining with the Order of Functions, we then reconnect with the Aezaiterian flow. The healing and loving presence there immerses us and helps us recover from the painful experience of entering the Order of Functions."

"What is the longest you have stayed there? —I hope you do not mind my questions?"

"Not at all. It helps to have someone to share it with. I do not know how long. Sometimes when we returned, we would find that much time had passed here. Other times, it was only moments."

"Where do you think you go when you enter the Order of Functions?"

"I do not think I go anywhere. If anything, it is not anywhere but everywhere. And nowhere. Again, words fail to serve this," Pan replied.

"Will you let me know ahead of time when you are going to engage in these fields?"

"That is an interesting term. Fields. What made you think of that?" Pan asked.

"I do not mean a field as in a meadow, but as in the vibrational lines of the vortex. The magnetic vortex winds its way throughout our world, yet it does not exist as such in a physical manner. Your description of your experience just somehow reminded me of that. But please, back to your plans—"

"There is a specific place allocated for this purpose; I am sure you have heard talk of it. When a Guardian executes his or her duties, guards are placed to protect the area from intrusion. Also, while I am in these fields, as you call them, my body remains in repose on Etera, unguarded and vulnerable."

"I see. Would you allow me to attend to you when you do this? By your own admission, you do not know how long you will be gone when you are engaged this way. I would like to stay by your side, just in case, and I will be there when you return to your body to let you know how much time has elapsed here."

Pan paced the room before answering. "I trust you, Tyria. I will accept your help. It comes not only from concern for the welfare of both my offling and me but also from your wisdom."

"You forgot the most important piece of it," Tyria said.

Pan looked at her.

"Love. Love is always the most important element. I care about you, Pan. You are the Guardian, our Leader, but you are also my friend. I would do anything to protect you," Tyria said softly.

Pan stood up, walked over, and pulled Tyria into her embrace. She leaned her head on Tyria's and said, "Thank you, my friend. I love you in return."

Having made her decision to fulfill her obligation as Guardian of Etera, Pan began preparing herself. She sought the Great Spirit in prayer and supplication. She repented of her stubbornness and refusal to accept the mantle of Guardianship. She spent long hours resting in the comfort and protection of Rohm'Mok's arms, trying to dispel the nearly constant exhaustion she endured. Until the day came when she felt it was time.

Accompanied by her mate, the most trusted guards, and Tyria, Pan made her way to the meadow above Kthama. It was late summer, and the sky was a deep blue, dotted with fluffy white clouds. The tall grasses and wildflowers rimmed the perimeter, filling the air with their sweet fragrance. Pan admired the beauty for a moment, guilt also once more rising at her neglect of her duties.

With the guards and Rohm'Mok in position, and after one last embrace with her mate, Pan left them at the perimeter, went into the sacred place within the center of the meadow, lay down in the soft grasses, and quietened her mind. Only Tyria was allowed to attend her and sat a short way from Pan's side.

As her father had taught her, Pan closed her eyes and sent her awareness down through her body, past the rich loam, the various striations of rock, down into the earth's magnetic core and into the rich vortex that was Etera's lifeblood. The moment she made contact, she was once again joined with joy itself, and indescribable pleasure coursed through every speck of her consciousness. It had been so long—too long. But this time, her father was not with her on this journey. In the past, she would find his consciousness and draw strength from his presence. But this time, there was no one. Basking in the delightful joining with the Aezaiteria, she reluctantly willed herself to move past the bliss of the creative life current to the place where her soul would be stretched apart and dispersed to the edges of infinity. She willed the strength to bear what came next when her very consciousness would be broken up and flung across eternity in a million bits. A place where solitude echoed down every corner of existence. Pan created her intention to enter the Order of Functions and accepted her mantle of service as the Guardian of Etera.

If time existed in the Order of Functions, in the next split-second, Pan learned that there were worse things than death. Far worse than the non-existence that the Order of Functions seemed to threaten to deliver at any moment. A fate worse than annihilation; in annihilation, at least there would be peaceful non-existence.

Tyria startled and jumped, rushing to Pan's side as the Guardian bolted to an upright sitting position, her eyes wide open and staring blankly, releasing a scream that echoed through the meadow and hillsides of Kthama and left Tyria chilled to the core of her soul.

The guards came running next, with Rohm'Mok at their side. He pushed past them and raced to Pan. "What is it? What is it?" he shouted as he grabbed her by the shoulders and shook her. Her eyes stared, unseeing, and he shook her again, "Pan, please, please. Come back to me. What is wrong?" he shouted at her, trying to make her hear him through the barrier of whatever had captured her mind. Perhaps even her soul.

In the next second, Pan looked into Rohm'Mok's eyes and then collapsed. Tyria came back to her side and tried to rouse her. Finally, after what felt like an eternity, Pan opened her eyes again. She looked up at

Rohm'Mok and then at her friend, the Healer, and broke down.

Rohm'Mok pulled her to him and encircled her with his arms. She clung to her mate, burying her face against his chest, and let out deep, wracking sobs, the depth of her heartache scarring their souls.

"By the love of the Great Spirit, *what is it*?" He was beside himself with panic. "What is wrong? What happened to you?"

Pan looked at him, her eyes bottomless wells of pain.

"Father," she gasped. She sobbed again, and Rohm'Mok held her tighter. The others silently waited for her to continue.

"Father did not return to the Great Spirit. He will never be reunited with my mother, my brothers, my sisters, or me. I tried. I tried my best. But I was powerless to free him. My father is trapped in the Order of Function *for all eternity*."

CHAPTER 11

L ife at Kayerm slowly returned to normal. With Nox'Tor gone, thoughts turned to how to make the best of their life there. Under Norland's kinder leadership, trust slowly started to develop between the males and females. A few more females chose mates, which was a cause of great celebration.

In the background, Kyana and Pagara continued to stay by Lorgil's side as much as they could. Lorgil steadfastly followed the Healer's prescription for complete bed rest until the offling was delivered and was very grateful to her friends for their care.

"We must also thank Wosot, who provides for us all," said Kyana. "Without his provision, we would have to be out foraging and would not be able to tend to you as we have."

"Wosot is a kind and gentle protector," Lorgil replied, looking directly at her.

Kyana said nothing.

"You could not ask for a better mate," Lorgil pressed on.

Kyana squeezed her eyes, shutting off the tears that had started to well in her eyes. Her thoughts returned to how carefully Wosot had carried Lorgil. How tender he was, with so much strength in that great frame and such a caring heart. In spite of her worry for her friend, she was jealous of how Lorgil had been so tenderly cradled in his arms. In that moment, she finally admitted to herself that she loved him.

"What is stopping you?" Lorgil brought herself up on one elbow. "I truly want to know. I have seen the way he looks at you and the way you look at him. We all have. If you are waiting for more time to pass since Nox'Tor's death, I assure you no one cares about that."

Kyana rubbed her hand over her face. "I do love him; I do," she admitted.

"Then what are you waiting for?" Lorgil asked again. Then her expression changed to shock. "Are you waiting for me to have my offling? Is that your concern? Are you afraid to enjoy happiness because of a fear about what might happen to me?"

Pagara looked at Kyana. "Is that it, Kyana? Please tell us."

Kyana covered her face with both hands and began to rock herself back and forth. Finally, she looked up and said to Lorgil, "How can I reach out for happiness for myself when yours, you who have become my dearest friend, hangs in the balance?"

The Healer moved closer to Kyana and put an arm around her.

"You must not let my challenges rob you of a chance for true joy in your life," Lorgil said. "Please do not do that. We each deserve to be happy, and the troubles of one should not keep another from finding her own joy. Please, do not keep your silence any longer. For one thing, Wosot is not getting any younger!"

Lorgil's remark was just what they all needed, and they laughed.

"There is more to it, though. I am troubled by confusion over my relationship with Nox'Tor. After he came to me that night at the fire and promised to try to win me back, I thought he had changed. It seemed he had. Perhaps, had I encouraged him more, we could have found our way back to one another."

Pagara and Lorgil looked at each other, and both frowned.

"I did not see a change in him," said the Healer. "From what I could see, he continued in his selfish ways. He made no effort to win you back. He was often sulking somewhere or else holed up in his quarters. I do not once remember him engaging with your offling. His words were just empty sounds in the wind."

"I did not see it, either," said Lorgil.

"Maybe you did not. But he did show kindnesses. Many times, when I returned to my quarters at the end of the day, I would find a special gift. Sometimes a freshly caught and prepared longfish, other times a pile of recently picked acorns. Now and then a pretty stone—and they were always my favorites. The colors I love most. He was showing me that he still cared and that he knew me well enough to know what pleased me." Kyana's voice dropped as she finished her story.

Pagara shook her head slowly, looking at Lorgil.

"Those gifts were not from Nox'Tor," Lorgil said, reaching out to take Kyana's hand. "It was Wosot who left them for you."

"What?" Kyana frowned. "No. Why do you say that?" She pulled her hand away.

"Because I saw him doing it, "said Lorgil. "I caught him many times giving those items to your daughters to place at your bedside. Sometimes I helped them by keeping watch for your return; if you doubt me, ask Lai. Seeing your happiness brought him joy. It does still. So, if that is what is confusing you—these kindnesses that you wrongly attributed to Nox'Tor—please, know that they came from Wosot."

"But I mentioned them to Nox'Tor, and he did not deny leaving them—" Then Kyana closed her eyes again. "Of course." She answered her own question. "Of course he would not. Nox'Tor would do just as he did, in silence take credit for them."

Kyana opened her eyes and looked at the two females who had become family to her. "My friends, my friends. What would I do without you?"

Lorgil smiled, "So what are you waiting for? Go and find him!"

Norland had gathered those whom he trusted most. In his circle sat Wosot, Toniss, and Trak. Had Pagara and Kyana not been busy, they would have been included.

"I am pleased that some of the females are selecting mates," he started off. "Perhaps we are on the path to healing as a community. And so perhaps the time has come to tend to matters of a more practical nature.

"Before our people left Kthama, there was agreement on the Sacred Laws. Rules to which we would all adhere to the end of enjoying a peaceful and ordered existence. Those laws must be kept alive; they must be freely spoken of and passed through the generations of our community, so they never pass from our memory. Let us discuss them now to confirm our agreement about what these laws were."

"I remember them well," said Toniss.

Silence fell as she recited the laws: *The needs of the community come first, before the need of any one individual. Honor females and do not subjugate them. Show humble forbearance for the failings of others. No hand must be raised to another except for protection or defense. Use the least amount of force necessary in conflict. Protect, heal, and shelter the sick, helpless, and those in need. Offling are our future and are sacred. Never take more than you need. No contact with outsiders, and never without consent.*"

"Those are the same I remember others reciting as well. I am relieved they live in our memory, intact. There was a story that the great Healer, Lor Onida, had recorded them on a scroll. I can only assume it is somewhere at Kthama," Norland added.

"In all our turmoil, I wonder how well the Sassen know these laws. Have they been ingrained in their memory as they are in the Mothoc's?" Trak asked.

"That is a good question," Norland replied. "One to which we must find the answer."

At Lorgil's urging, Kyana was out looking for Wosot and finally spotted him walking back toward Kayerm accompanied by Toniss, Trak, and Dotrat. Her heart pounded as she watched them come toward her. They were talking among themselves as they walked and had not noticed her. Then, Wosot lifted his head, and with each further step, he kept his eyes locked on hers.

Kyana felt her heart racing more quickly. She clenched and unclenched her fists, trying to relax.

He was just a male; why was she acting like this? Oh, but he was not; he was not just any male.

Within a few moments, the group had caught up to her. As it was obvious what was passing between Wosot and Kyana, the others moved on, smiling, and left the two to each other.

"I— I— Lorgil is resting, and I thought I would take a walk," Kyana managed to stammer.

Wosot took a step closer to her—uncomfortably close. "Is that what you were doing?"

Kyana could see him looking down at her, from her eyes to her lips, and back up to meet her gaze.

"Out for a walk?" he repeated, then reached up, and his hand grazed the side of her face; she could feel her cheeks burning.

"Yes. No, I— I am glad to see you. I wanted to thank you for saving us from Nox'Tor back there. If it were not for you—"

He was so close; the heat from his body was inflaming the longing she felt for him. She wanted to wrap her arms around his neck and press her lips to his.

He gently raised her chin with his hand. "Never doubt that I will care for you and that I will protect you and your offling until my last dying breath."

Then he leaned down enough to kiss her sweetly on her forehead. "I must be off to my duties. Meet me at the evening fire tonight, if you can?"

As he walked away, Kyana steadied herself. Her knees were suddenly weak.

That night, after making sure her daughters were settled down, and Lorgil was cared for, Kyana went to join the others at the evening fire.

The scent of the burning wood mingled with the night air was comforting and so pleasant. The twinkling stars in the clear sky overhead reminded them of the glory of creation and the loving hand of the Great Spirit, who had created it all.

Wosot was sitting next to Norland, deeply immersed in storytelling while the others around the fire listened intently. Kyana stayed back, not wanting to interrupt. At the end of the story, everyone laughed outright and slapped each other on the knees. As the laughter faded, Wosot noticed Kyana standing there and waved her over to sit next to him.

He looked at her briefly, smiled, and handed her his stick so she could poke at the fire. She laughed and playfully gave it a try, sending embers floating skyward.

"I am glad you came," Wosot said. Then he reached his arm behind Kyana and pulled her closer until she was pressed up against his side.

A shockwave went through her. "Oh."

Wosot looked at her and smiled, then looked at her lips again and back up to meet her gaze.

"You are teasing me," she whispered, smiling.

"Well, I am certainly trying to." He smiled in return.

She looked down and took his hand, and laced her fingers through his. Wosot brought their hands up and kissed the back of hers lightly, allowing his lips to linger a moment.

He leaned over and whispered in her ear, "When you are ready, and only when you are ready, I will still be waiting for you."

His warm breath on her neck sent a chill through her, and she felt her insides twist with desire for him. Suddenly, she remembered that they were not alone. She opened her eyes and looked around to see the others at the circle grinning at both of them, some nodding and casting glances at each other.

Embarrassed at their public display but pleased to see that the others appeared approving, she excused herself and went to her quarters. Careful not to wake Lorgil or her daughters, she slid quietly onto her sleeping mat.

But sleep was not to come that night; Kyana could not get thoughts of Wosot out of her mind.

Back at Kthama, Pan lay in the Healer's Quarters. She had not spoken since her words in the meadow, after which Rohm'Mok carefully carried her back and placed her in Tyria's care. He stayed by her side as much as possible.

They all waited for Pan to come out of her silence.

In the hallway outside the Healer's Quarters, Rohm'Mok asked Tyria if there was nothing more she could do.

Tyria shook her head; her heart was breaking. "I love her too. If there were anything else I knew to do, a secret to unturn, I would move the mountains that cradle Kthama. She will not eat. She still does not speak. Honestly, I fear for her life and for the life of your offling."

Filled with despair, Rohm'Mok leaned against the rock wall. He felt beaten, lost, powerless to save her as the love of his life faded in front of his eyes.

"It is out of my hands," Tyria continued softly. "I am afraid that only the mercy of the Great Spirit can save Pan."

Rohm'Mok looked at her. "Thank you for all you are doing. I never meant to imply I doubted you."

Rohm'Mok made his way to the sacred meadow above Kthama. The place where Pan and all the Guardians before her engaged the Aezaitera. The same place where Pan had just discovered that her father was trapped in the Order of Functions.

Rohm'Mok walked to the spot where he had last held his beloved, just before she slipped into unconsciousness, and dropped to his knees. He lifted his eyes to the clear blue sky overhead and spoke into the sudden silence of the meadow.

"I have come to this sacred place, the place of my mate Pan and her father before her. The place where every Guardian who has protected Etera and served you has come to carry out their service to you. Please, Great Spirit, hear my prayer.

"Through the years, I longed to find love. Many females sought me out; you know this. But I waited, standing on the promise you placed in my heart— that there would be one who would return my love in the way that the legends say Moc'Tor loved E'ranale. And then, finally, you brought Pan to me and me to her.

"I am not a Guardian. I am not even much of a Leader. I am just a male who is bowed here before you, begging you to return to me the one I would exchange my life for. I know I have no right to enter this sacred meadow. But I am here, on my knees. I am begging you not to take the one who means everything to me. I need her. Our offling needs her. And Etera needs her."

Silence still filled the meadow. Overhead, a single black crow looked down, tilting its head back and forth as it watched the Mothoc male kneeling in this most sacred place of the Guardians.

Rohm'Mok returned to the Healer's Quarters to find Tyria sitting on the edge of Pan's sleeping mat.

"Please, tell me she is going to be alright," Rohm'Mok said—again.

"The next day or so will tell us. She is nearly at a point of no return. If her current direction does not change, she may lose your offling. Or we may lose them both. At this point, it will take a miracle.

"I will leave you alone with her, but I will check back in a while. Maybe if you stay here, it will help." And Tyria left to make arrangements for a sleeping mat to be placed next to Pan's.

While Tyria was gone, Rohm'Mok sat next to his mate. Yet again, he picked up one of her hands in his, "I know you can hear me. You must live. You must live for me; you must live for our offling. You must live because you are the Guardian, and you are Etera's only hope. I love you so much, and I cannot bear to lose you. Please, please fight to stay with me. Please."

He stretched out next to Pan, and snuggled her up next to him with her head resting on his shoulder. He pulled the cover up and held her gently, praying again to the Great Spirit not to take her from him.

⁂

In the Corridor, E'ranale turned to the magnificent, shimmering male standing next to her. The same male who had spoken to Pan's father before he returned to the Chamber of the Ancients and entered the Order of Functions.

"It is time to bring her to me," she said.

(✦)

Pan looked around. She found herself back in the sacred meadow above Kthama. Only it was far more than that. She frowned, trying to understand what was happening. Everything looked the same, yet it was imbued with a concentration of life she had never before experienced. The colors were so vibrant, the birdsong in the background sweeter, more lilting than any she had ever heard. The grass beneath her feet seemed to welcome her as if it were holding her in its embrace. It was a place of unspeakable glory and grace beyond understanding. *Where am I? Am I dead? Have I left Etera to join with the Great Spirit?*

A light began to appear in front of her. Slowly, it took form.

Pan's jaw dropped, and her eyes opened wide as she recognized the figure materializing. "Mother! Mother!" she exclaimed. "Is it really you?"

She ran to E'ranale and was caught up in her embrace.

"Oh, my darling daughter. How long I have waited to hold you again. Yes. It is me. Take comfort in knowing that it is truly your mother who stands before you."

"But where are we? Am I dead?"

"We are in what is called the Corridor," E'ranale

explained. "It is but one step in the return to the Great Spirit. And no, you are not dead. I have brought you, the true part of yourself, here to me. Your body lies back in Etera's realm, watched over and cared for by those there who love you so much."

Pan looked down at her body; she ran her hands over her arms, touched her face. "It feels real, and yet so much more than that. This feels more real than anything I have ever experienced before."

"That is because you have shifted one vibration closer to the Great Spirit, which is the source of all creation, of all truth. And when you are standing in truth, you are standing in the presence of the One-Who-Is-Three."

"Will I join you here one day? After I die?" she asked.

"Yes. You will join me one day, never to be parted again," E'ranale answered.

"So, all those who have returned to the Great Spirit are also here?" Pan asked as she looked around. "But what about Father? Where is Father?!"

"Not all are here," E'ranale answered. "Your father is not here, Pan. That is why I have brought you to me. There is much I need to explain, much that will help you understand the importance of what lies ahead that is alone yours to do.

"Look at me. Your father's body is with mine and Straf'Tor's, deep within Kthama Minor in the Chamber of the Ancients. In time, it will be discovered by others, but for now, its secrets are safe, locked away with the shame of the Age of Darkness. Straf'Tor and I entered the Corridor when our bodies perished on Etera. That was not the case with your father. His body perished after he abandoned it, when he sent his consciousness, his very being, into the Order of Functions."

"Oh, yes. I— I entered the Order of Functions. I sensed him there. Oh, Mother—"

"Your father knew it was what he had to do. He could not let you bear alone the burden of what he had set in motion. He knew that what faces you will be more than anyone could handle alone. Not even Moc'Tor himself, if fate had put him in your place. He serves the Great Spirit in the Order of Functions to relieve the strain on you so that you, in turn, may fulfill this destiny."

"I tried! I tried, but I was not powerful enough to free him. Forever. He is trapped forever in that place of—of existence yet non-existence." Pan covered her face with her hands.

"I understand your grief—I bear it as well. But all is not lost; there is a way to free Moc'Tor. What falls to you to do will set the course for his release, and you will not be alone. In time, the Promised One will come. He will be known as the Seventh of the Six. When he takes his place, he will usher in the Wrak-Ashwea, the Age of Light. He will be the first Akassa Guardian to walk Etera. And you, Pan, will be his teacher."

"An Akassa Guardian? And *I* will teach this

Promised One? How is that possible? I feel I am barely handling what is on my shoulders now."

"There are many events that must take place in a certain order before any of this comes to pass. You have centuries to grow in your abilities, many of which you have not yet discovered. When the An'Kru, the Promised One, arrives on Etera, you will be ready to train him. Until then, you must be strong —for yourself, for Rohm'Mok, for your offling, for your father. For all of Etera. You must fully accept your mantle of the Guardianship of Etera."

Pan hung her head in shame, admitting the struggle within herself to accept her role was not over.

"Our time here is almost up. But, before we part, I must tell you about the Leader's Staff. Within a chamber at the top is a crystal. Tremendous power lies in that crystal, and it was given only to the House of 'Tor.

"As you know, it is sacrilege for anyone other than a Leader to touch a Leader's Staff, or for any Leader to touch the staff of another. This creates reverence for the position of Leader while concealing the existence of the crystal. If any other Leader were to handle the 'Tor staff, the difference in heft and balance between it and his would be obvious. And conversely, you are not aware of the difference since you have never held any other, either. This sacred crystal is irreplaceable, and when the An'Kru comes to Etera, he will need it when he frees your father."

E'ranale reached out and touched her daughter's face. "Return to your body. Rest. Heal. You come from greatness, and there is greatness in you. Continue in your wisdom about what must come for the Akassa and for the Mothoc. Most of all, Pan, trust yourself. In time, before you put in motion the final steps of what you will realize has to be done, you must go to Kayerm."

Despite the beauty of the Corridor, despite her mother's loving presence, Pan was alarmed.

E'ranale continued, "You must tell our people, the Mothoc at Kayerm, that they must hand over the leadership to the Sassen. As for the Sassen themselves, remind them of the Rah-hora. Remind them of their duty to avoid the Akassa, lest the Sassen themselves be destroyed. Tell them they must keep the Mothoc culture alive in preparation for the age to come. Finally, you must teach the Sassen Leader to perform the One Mind, the knowledge of which must be passed down from one Leader to the next. Other knowledge will be given to them at the appropriate time."

E'ranele stood looking at her daughter. "How I wish I could keep you here with me forever. But not yet. In time, you will join me here in the Corridor, and you will rest once again in my arms. But now, it is time for you to return to your body. When you awake back on Etera, you will know what is yours to do."

Off in the distance, Pan saw a small figure forming. "Mother, who is that?"

E'ranale turned to see who was approaching. "My darling Pan, I had hoped another path would be possible. Prepare yourself."

"Who is it?" Pan asked again as the figure approached closer.

"That, beloved, is your daughter."

Pan watched as the figure of a young female approached. She studied the dark, deep-set eyes and the dark coat with a silver upper aspect similar to that of Dak'Tor. Pan could see the influence of both herself and Rohm'Mok. In a place of no-time, it still felt that it took an eternity for the figure to reach her.

She could only stare, not sure what to say.

"Hello, Mama."

E'ranale looked at her daughter, frozen in uncertainty. "Pan," she said, snapping the Guardian out of her stupor. "This is your daughter, Tala."

Pan stammered, "Is she—?"

"No. She is not dead. Though in your timeline on Etera she is not yet born, her true essence exists here. But the fact that she has come to us does not speak well of the potentiality for her life on Etera."

"What does that mean," asked Pan, unable to take her eyes off Tala.

"You are not well; your body is in a state of fatigue and exhaustion. You have neglected your duties to the Aezaiterian flow, which serves Etera but also serves to strengthen you and maintain your health. Remember that a Guardian is practically immortal because of the life-giving force of the Aezaiteria. But you have been negligent in that."

"Are you saying that I may lose her? That Tala may not be born?" Pan asked, turning her gaze to her mother.

"The future is not set, daughter. If you do not turn the current state around, yes, you may lose her. You can see that the day will come when you will know her here, but you may never see her grow up and live her life on Etera."

Pan stared at Tala, who remained silent. "I will not lose you, Tala. I promise I will turn away from neglecting my health."

Then she looked at her mother. "I have failed in my responsibilities as Guardian. My anger at your passing, and what I felt was my father's betrayal by making me Leader of the High Rocks—I have let them rule me. I am sorry. I am so sorry."

E'ranale stepped forward and put her arms around her daughter. "The Great Spirit knows your heart, Pan. Return to Etera. Renew your commitment to living. Turn your soul's intention toward living. And then do your best from now on. The Akassa need you. The Sarnonn need you. The Others need you. And the Mothoc need you. You have much yet to accomplish; the future of Etera rests on your shoulders and your ability to trust The Order of Functions."

Pan took another look at Tala, who was smiling at

her warmly. She reached out her arms, and her daughter stepped into them. "I will do everything I can to give you life—and as wonderful a life as I can create for you," Pan whispered into her daughter's ear.

"I know you will, Mama," Tala said before stepping back.

"Now, you must return," E'ranale said softly.

Pan nodded and created her intention to return to her body on Etera.

CHAPTER 12

The two sentries Hatos'Mok had sent out at the Guardian's request were on their way back to the Deep Valley. They had been gone for several months, following the currents of the vortex snaking across Etera. They had set out south, then west, and then turned far north. Discovering what they believed was that which they had been sent to find, they made their way back toward the Deep Valley, happy to be bringing good news.

"I will be glad to get back to a routine," said Asolp.

B'Hit agreed. "Familiar hunting areas, waterways, gathering sites. A much easier life than this one of wandering about."

Suddenly Asolp stopped. "Something is wrong."

"I feel it too. It is out of our way, but we must investigate it."

The two giant males set out in the direction of the disturbance they had sensed.

Off in the distance, nestled under an outcropping of rock, there looked to be an entrance to a cave. As they walked, their discomfort increased.

"Great sadness here," Asolp said. "Terrible loss. And also deep anger."

Before long, they were at the cave's entrance. They carefully went in and soon found they could go no further. A heavy tumble of rocks and boulders blocked the way.

"There were Mothoc here," commented Asolp. "It feels as if they lived here not that long ago."

B'Hit walked over and picked up a piece of crushed material. "A water gourd, or at least what is left of it." He kicked at some rubble and found another piece. "This is clearly our design. The Others do not use such large and heavy materials."

"Nor do they live in caves."

"Whoever they were, they are long gone. Yet the imprint of their grief and anger remains." B'Hit tossed away the piece of gourd. "We must leave this place. But before we go, let us say a prayer to the Great Spirit for healing for those who have suffered such a terrible event."

"Who were they, and where did they go?" wondered Asolp. "Most likely, we will never know."

The two spent a moment in silence before continuing on their way to the Deep Valley, now with even more information to bring to Hatos'Mok.

Pan realized that her mate was holding her. She reached up and touched his face. Rohm'Mok's eyes flew open, and he turned, careful not to dislodge her.

"You are awake! How do you feel?" he asked, clasping her fingers.

"I am tired. I feel as if I have been sleeping forever," she said quietly. "How long has it been since I went to the meadow?"

"I do not even want to tell you. Tyria said it will not be that long before you deliver our offling."

Pan was shocked at his words. Then she reached down and touched her belly. "Is she alright?"

"Yes. Our offling is fine. But, *she*?" Rohm'Mok smiled. "Is there something you are not telling me?"

"I have so much to share with you," Pan answered. "But first, I realize I have neglected my duties as Guardian. I have let my anger derail me from my calling. I am going to stop fighting everything now, I promise. I do not want to lose you or our offling."

"Rest," Rohm'Mok said, easing himself from next to her. "Tyria will want to know you have returned to us. I will be right back."

Pan lay on the mat, thinking. *My father. Trapped in the Order of Functions. In that place of no place.* But at least now she had hope. And she vowed she would do everything she could to fulfill her duties as Guardian of Etera. Suddenly, a sharp pain shot through her. Pan's hands instinctively went to her belly. *Oh please, Great Spirit, please. Please do not let my stubbornness cost Tala her life on Etera.*

Sent under the orders of the Guardian to locate another underground cave system in close proximity to a strong magnetic vortex, Asolp and B'Hit returned to the Deep Valley having completed their mission. Bakru immediately sent for Hatos'Mok and his son, Bahr'Mok, now Leader of the Deep Valley.

Both listened intently as Asolp explained first about the expansive cave system they had found sitting on a rich magnetic vortex, just as the Guardian had hoped.

"It is quite far north," B'Hit reported. "The air seemed cooler there, which would benefit us in the hot weather. There is a rich stream that snakes around the base of the mountainside. There are also many deer and rich meadows full of the Great Spirit's blessings. Clearly, it is as hospitable as the High Rocks and the Deep Valley."

"As for the vortex there, I would say it is nearly as powerful as the one under Kthama," B'Hit added.

"Thank you. We must get this information to the Guardian," said Bahr'Mok.

"There is more, Adik'Tar," Asolp said. "We took a circuitous route back. On the way, we found what I am sure is an abandoned Mothoc colony with the entrance blocked by a cave-in. We could not tell how long ago they abandoned it, nor where they went."

"The despair lingered, Adik'Tar," added B'Hit. "But more than that. There was great anger, resentment, bitterness over the loss of loved ones in the disaster. Wherever they went, the surviving Mothoc, I think we must be concerned for their state of mind."

Bahr'Mok told them that he would prepare a messenger to go immediately to Kthama.

"No," Hatos'Mok said. "I will go myself. I wish to discover if there is anything else the Guardian requires.

"Now, both of you start over and tell us every detail of both places you found."

After Asolp and B'Hit had finished and been dismissed, Bahr'Mok turned to Hatos'Mok. "What does this mean, Father?"

"It means that though the Age of Wrak-Wavara has come to an end, locked within Kthama Minor, there are still debts to be paid for our betrayal of the Others so long ago. I fear that the hearts of the Mothoc will, for a little longer, be denied the peace we crave."

With a heavy heart, Hatos'Mok placed his hand on his son's shoulder. "Lead Awenasa well, my son, and cherish each day sheltered here within her walls. I will return as soon as I can."

With that, Hatos'Mok left his home, in the back of his mind fearing that he knew the sacrifice the Guardian would, in time, call on them all to make.

PLEASE READ

Thank you for reading Book Two. I hope that means you will continue with Book Three: The Secret of The Leader's Staff! Following Book Three will be Book Four and Book Five. After that I am not sure. We'll see so stay the course with me please.

At this point if you have not read Series One, you may be inclined to just skip it. But I encourage you read it. Series One, Wrak-Ayya: The Age of Shadows, covers the journey of the People thousands and thousands of years following what takes place in this series. There are many answered questions from Series One, in Series Two. Aren't you curious what you are missing lol?

Want to stay informed? There are several handy ways:

Please follow me on Amazon on my author page.

Or you can subscribe to my newsletter at: https://www.subscribepage.com/theeterachronclessubscribe

I also have a private Facebook group called The Etera Chronicles

If you enjoyed this book, please leave a positive review or at least a positive rating. Of course, five stars are the best.

But, if you found fault with it, please email me directly and tell me your viewpoint. I do want to know.

You can find the link to leave a product review on

the book link on Amazon, where you purchased the book.

Positive reviews on Goodreads are also greatly appreciated.

I wish you well and I hope you continue with me on this journey of What If?

Blessings - Leigh

ACKNOWLEDGMENTS

Having written thirteen books now, I have to once again acknowledge my dear husband who has sacrificed many many hours of our personal time together so I could continue my author career.

My wonderful editor Joy who never fails me.

My dear friend Carolene.

Also, my little pack of Pomeranians who patiently nap around me while I peck away at the keyboard.

And, my beloved brother Richard, who continues to be my biggest supporter.

I love you all.

Now and forever.

Made in the USA
Las Vegas, NV
20 February 2024

86028831R00163